Why I Blame Trump On Jesus

And Other Things I Don't Dare Say Out Loud

Selina Rosen

JUST CAUSE

An imprint of
Yard Dog Press

Why I Blame Trump on Jesus and Other Things I Can't Say Out Loud
Selina Rosen
First Edition Copyright © Selina Rosen, 2020

Published under "Just Cause," an imprint of Yard Dog Press

ISBN 978-1-945941-25-2
Why I Blame Trump on Jesus and Other Things I Can't Say Out Loud
First Edition Copyright © Selina Rosen, 2020

Yard Dog Press
710 W. Redbud Lane
Alma, AR 72921-7247

http://www.yarddogpress.com

Edited by Selina Rosen
Copy Editor & Technical Editor Lynn Rosen
Cover art by Melanie Miller Fletcher

First Edition March 15, 2020
Printed in the United States of America
0 9 8 7 6 5 4 3 2 1

Dedication

For my therapist's kids.

I'm putting them through college. I might as well dedicate a book to them, too.

Table of Contents

Dedication iii

Chapter One 1

Chapter Two..13

Chapter Three 19

Chapter Four 23

Chapter Five 29

Chapter Six 39

Chapter Seven 57

Chapter Eight 71

Chapter Nine 85

Chapter Ten 105

Chapter Eleven..125

Chapter Twelve 149

Chapter Thirteen 163

Chapter Fourteen..187

Chapter Fifteen 197

About the Author vii

About the Cover Artist ix

Yard Dog Press Titles as Of This Print Date xi

Chapter One

"I blame Trump on Jesus," I tell my therapist.

Her usual cool, noncommittal demeanor erodes into a temporary mask of *'What the fuck?!'* She has her cool back before she asks, "Why is that?"

"Come on it's obvious the Jesus-jammers wanted him in," and even as I am saying this in the closed walls of the therapist's office I'm wondering if it is really safe because I know she is a Christian, and even though she was recommended to me by the "agency" because she is more liberal and broad minded than most of the people in this little slice of Bible Belt hell we call Jakeville, I wonder how much I can say before she judges me and finds me wanting like everyone else I have ever had anything at all to do with. I want to leave it at that, but of course a therapist never gets more excited than they do when they can tell someone is holding back.

"Why did they want him in?"

All great writers have one thing in common—or so I am told—they are willing—as I have heard so many times that hearing it now puts my teeth on edge—to 'open a vein and bleed all over the page'. In other words, they tell the truth. There is an honesty with which they tell a story. They are willing to say those things that people think but never say out loud, but are they really? I contend that *most* of what we think we wouldn't dare to speak out loud which means... everything we say is just crap that was cleaned up to make things more palatable to the masses—who only really want crap. What is the point of being in therapy if even there I won't say the things I can't say anywhere else? So I fire at will.

"Because they hate everyone and everything that isn't them. He said he hated everyone and everything that they do, and so they knocked each other out of the way to vote for him as quick as they could. They are way too stupid to understand that they will be the first ones screwed over by Big Money. They waded right in and willingly 'drank the red stuff' because he was promising to build a wall, put blacks and homos in their place, and keep the Muslims from bombing us...."

After that I got more rabidly anti-Christian, but a lot less articulate. After all I am a gay Jew living in Jesus Land. I explain how they have all this Muslim hate going on and want to point out every act of violence any Muslim terrorist has ever committed while they forget the generations of crimes the KKK has committed against anyone who isn't the right color or even the right kind of Christian. Meanwhile the lord's army mutilates, rapes, and kills people in the Congo using the illegal Ivory trade to fund their war against... I'm not even sure they know who. They never mention Christian involvement in the rape of South America, The Spanish Inquisition, the atrocities of the Crusades, or the Holocaust. They ignore the Catholics fighting with Protestants and generations of whoever was in charge oppressing the other. In other words, I gave her the whole *spiel* I usually keep in my head.

I end with, "Christians want to point their fingers at Muslim extremists and act like they represent all Muslims, but when someone who claims they are Christian commits a horrid atrocity they say they aren't really Christian and they don't own any part of it. They don't accept that their doctrine led these people to act in these hideous ways. They have no problem blaming Islam for what a handful of extremists do, but they don't own their own crimes at all."

She takes a deep breath and says calmly, "Just like no one ever paid for what happened to you, all the things you have gone through and are going through?"

"I just don't see why everyone gets a pass but me. My feet get held to the fire for everything I ever did... everyone who hurts me gets a pass... no, worse than that, they get elevated. My ex-husband does horrible things to me. He gets everything and my son thinks he is a small god. He has been telling everyone that he is at death's door for ten years now. He says jump and my son asks how high and how far for ten years. Sometimes I wonder if he is sick at all because he is and always has been a master manipulator. He lies more easily than most people tell the truth. He plays pathetic pretty well. If he ever does die he will die with a lie on his lips and will never ever apologize or admit to all the horrible crimes he has committed against... everyone who ever came into contact with him and... I'm the bad guy."

"I want you to make a list of all the things you feel responsible for and bring it to your next visit."

The problem with therapy is that they don't give you any answers they expect you to come up with the answers yourself. They send you home to think about what you told them. On a good week they give you some sort of homework which you don't think will help but somehow does. After a couple of years I still couldn't really tell you why.

Being task driven, I start making that list as soon as I get home. I almost stop and throw it away because my very first thought is... *Everything, I'm responsible for everything.* Keeping the house, taking care of the live-stock, planting and caring for the garden and the yard, my grandson, my wife, the people I go to Temple with. The fate of the planet...

My grandson. Mostly I feel responsible for him. This is just one of the reasons I am in therapy because you see he has become my whole life. I have mostly raised him for most of his life and now the kids decide to move to another town and I went from seeing him every day to seeing him two or three times a month if I'm lucky and...

How do I take care of my grandson now? How do I protect him?

See my son and his family lived next door for the last nine years which was good because the first three years of Avy's life my son was addicted to prescription pain killers and worked sixty hours a week. His lovely wife was on prescription pain killers, smoked a shit load of pot, drank, and didn't want to raise a kid.

She was a stay-at-home mom, but her baby was here most of the time. And I was fine with that because from the moment I first saw Avy I was in love. He wasn't a week old when the publishing house I wrote for imploded. 2009 was a really bad year for the book biz, publishing houses were blowing up everywhere and... Long story short, when the house went under everyone else either had their agents find them a new house to work for or got agents to help them find a new house. I made the decision to try to work on my own so that I could help raise my grandson.

See I knew I made mistakes with my son, but I have always loved babies and kids. I was a better person than I was when I was young; I had more patience and could do a better job. Since Jenny seemed more interested in just about everything than caring for Avy, it seemed like I was getting a second chance to raise a kid. At the very least he needed me.

Now Jenny was all about telling the world how much she loved Avy and how much she loved being a mom... and it was true. As an *idea* she loved it, but in *practice* not so much. She needed a whole lot of "me" time and "couple" time, and not a whole lot of actual "taking care of the baby" time.

And that was before she decided she needed something that was just for her and started the first of dozens of jobs. She would work till they were done with her or she was done with them. We could never make real plans to do anything. We would have Avy three or four days in a row including overnight because she wouldn't be feeling well. We would have him whenever he was sick or teething or they were in rehab—which they did twice before it stuck—I got him off the bus ever since he started school and he would stay here till she came home—whenever that was.

I happily gave up the career I had worked my whole life for to take care of my grandson, because after all it wasn't doing what I wanted it to do anyway and again I felt needed. I wanted to protect him from having the kind of childhood I had or even the one I gave his father. But I never had a say in what they do with him.

Now that they have moved Jenny calls all the shots. Sometimes she is there when he gets off the bus; sometimes he comes home to an empty house. I never know where he is or what is happening to him. I can't protect him, and it is driving me nuts—which wasn't a very long ride.

One day I was supposed to pick him up when he got off the bus. He was supposed to but he didn't. When I called to make sure someone had him, Jenny said he had gotten off the bus at Jason's house and she was sure she had told me he would.

She didn't tell me and she knows she didn't. It is a game she likes to play—push all my buttons and see if I will scream. My little sister, Ellen, tells me I win when I don't yell at her.

It does not feel like winning.

Liz gets home from work. I'm cooking dinner. I grunt in her general direction; she grunts back. After twenty-five years together, going through the problems of raising her manipulative, selfish, alcoholic son from her marriage to a man and my addicted, selfish son from my marriage to a man—as well as hot and cold running menopause, my failed career and her stress-filled one—we had run out of pleasantries. We would sometimes go two months without having sex and sometimes just trying to talk to her about anything made me feel like a sword was over my head.

And she was getting ready to retire and how the hell was that going to work if we could barely stand each other now?

I was depressed... No, fuck that, I was having the mother, farther, and second cousin twice removed of all PTSD episodes, and it just wasn't letting up. There was nothing that broke through my dread but Avy, and... they were taking him away in stages and I had NO control. None.

For someone with PTSD, a situation where they have no control sends them into a near if not total panic, and I had recently come to the spiritual realization that control is an illusion which... AHHHH!

Liz and I had been through highs and lows in our relationship dozens of times. Just like straight people all our real problems centered around finances and the fucking kids.

That night we ate dinner, exchanged hellos and half-assed kisses on the cheek and went to separate parts of the house.

See I run the show. Liz has never—and I admit it now—never will be able to pick up the slack. You might as well cut the line because if things are left up to her nothing, nothing at all, will be done. She is five years older than me, and at sixty-four just getting through a day of teaching college freshmen leaves her with nothing left to give. Me... well, I'm way too needy. I needed someone who I felt had my back. I had given up completely on her ability to actually do something to lift me from my depression. She has no idea what to do if I don't start everything. I have to *start* sex, I have to *make plans* to do things and if I don't... we half-watch TV and eat in the living room and go to bed in separate beds—because she moved out of our bed during her menopause and now I can't sleep through her snoring which has gotten so bad it sounds like she's running a chainsaw.

So my career was over, my marriage was mostly dead, I was in the worst depression of my life—which makes it monumental—and if all that wasn't bad enough, possibly the last person who should be in *any* responsible position was president.

I was in therapy because I had no friends I could tell any of the things I needed to say. I could afford therapy only because the laws had changed so that I could legally marry Liz and be on her insurance. Now who knew when the Trump mobile was going to roll right over the rights we had just gotten?

I blame Jesus!

You can't say things like you got married to get a break on your taxes or to get insurance without people losing their fucking minds. There is nothing remotely romantic about reality after all. When we got legally married we had already been together for twenty-four years. Our kids had already beaten every single trace of spontaneity and romance from our lives, and what they hadn't destroyed, raising a grandkid had.

We were old, but here's what I remember about getting married—Liz came running into the living room and announces, "You have to marry me!"

I'm like, "Why? Are you pregnant?"

That was when I found out about the Supreme Court ruling which... Well we hadn't even known it was in the cards. There had been so much hysterical yelling and the Christian Right screaming that sweet baby Jesus the god of love was causing hurricanes to ravage any place remotely inclusive of gays that we never thought it would happen in our life-times. Of course this ass-backwards state still wasn't marrying "them queers," so we went to Iowa. I remember that trip—and that it was mostly Liz crying a lot and me thinking I might finally be able to get insurance and wondering how much it was going to save us on our taxes (which turned out to be nothing at all).

But a few months later when we were married in our yard by a rabbi in front of only the friends and family we had that supported us as a couple.... Well, that was the first and, to date, *only* time in my life where my head was in a good enough place that I didn't have any preconceived notions about how it should be. I made plans; I didn't worry if they didn't work. When problems arose I took care of them to the best of my ability and didn't care if things were just how I wanted them. It was a true celebration of the love we had for each other. It was as close to perfect as anything in my life has ever been.

At that moment we were in sync, closer than we had ever been. We'd lived through hell to be together at a time before anyone was on board and in an area where most people still hate us because of who and what we are. That hasn't changed nor do I think it ever will because... Fundies love nothing more than to hate, and we are surrounded by fundies.

Don't know what a fundy is? It's *any* fundamentalist religious nut job of *any* faith who thinks it's their duty to make other people unhappy by judging them and finding them hated by God.

Why am I such a fucking mess now? Because I had it all figured out. My son and the twisted woman beast he married had kept me jumping for years. Yet in the middle of it all I had found a way to enjoy myself, to be alright with my lot in life in a way I never really had been able to do before. When Liz and I got married I had it all figured out, all of it, and I was happy with where I was so all the horrible things that brought me to that moment... I was alright with them.

Here's a truth: horrible people never let you keep those moments of peace. In fact, they can't stand to see anyone happy. They just can't.

My ex-husband Levi was just that sort of person. The pictures of our wedding went up on Facebook and he just couldn't help himself, he had to fire at will. Not because I had married a woman, no he threw a wall-eyed fit because I wore tallit—the shawl with fringes that Jews wear to pray and at special occasions. See he was raised

Orthodox and in his opinion women were to be treated as unclean, stupid vessels for a man's pleasure. Most real Orthodox folks are not that misogynistic. But you see Levi and his family were that rare breed of northeast coast "Orthodox" who ate pork and shellfish, did whatever they wanted in their personal lives, had no business ethics, only attended Temple on the High Holy days, and the only thing remotely Jewish they did in their home was light Chanukah candles. Yet they damned the Conservative branch of Judaism for not doing things "correctly" and the Reform movement...? Well they were just wrong about everything.

I'm a Reform Jew.

He proceeded to argue with all my friends at length. Finally one friend said, "It's really none of your business." At which point he went into a rant about how it was his business because I was raising his grandson to believe this same bullshit. You know... that women were equal to men.

How dare I?

Now is probably a good time to tell you that Levi had become a born again Christian twenty years before this. In fact, he got up on the pulpit in his Bible-thumping church one Sunday morning "when moved by the spirit" and preached about how Jesus had saved him from a meaningless life as a Jew. He was fond of telling people that he was a "complete" Jew... You know because he found Jesus.

Really? The Christians have got to stop hiding their god so that he is so hard to find!

As he had done to every group of people he had ever been associated with, Levi soon had that whole church at each-others' throats and had swindled half of them out of large sums of cash. Half the congregation, including the preacher, had been driven out and he was now their full-time pastor. And how did I know all of this? Because his wife's uncle had been their preacher and he came to Avy's birthday party one year (Levi didn't; he was on a cruise that year) and he was all about telling everyone who would listen just exactly how Levi had wronged him and other members of the congregation.

I was all for it until the asshole said, "It was because he was a Jew. Once a Jew always a Jew and those people are crooked."

"Really?" I said. "Because Levi's Jewish education began and ended at being sent to summer camp every year for two weeks and he didn't even *bar mitzvah*. He half-assed knew some of the prayers, he never studied a word of *Torah*, and he never studied Jewish ethics."

My son got mad at me for causing a scene and asked me to leave.

See what I'm dealing with?

If my son heard one word his stepmother's uncle said he didn't believe any of it, and when I think about it the preacher was probably purposely not saying anything in my son's hearing. The problem is I am normally loud, so when someone says something like that and I am pissed off I get really loud. So likely as not the only person my son heard say disparaging things about his father that day was me.

Here is my mistake—a mistake I have made many times with my son. I took the Facebook posts down because I didn't want Ryan to see what an asshole his father was. There are many times when I should have let my son see the truth of that man but didn't, and now I pay for it. Ryan thinks I was always bad mouthing his dad, but I didn't. I rarely said anything hateful about the bastard to Ryan, and when I did... I never came close to telling him what a bastard Levi was, not even *close*.

As they say nice guys finish last.

See I have become the villain in Ryan's life story. The mean, frustrated dyke that abused his poor, poor father, a saintly man with a halo walking on feet of gold.

I have read a mountain of self-help books and studied theological texts at length. You know what none of the books talk about? How you find balance when you have mediocrity and horrible crap. When you never actually win at a fucking thing and have to settle, always settle, for what you can get instead of what you actually want and then... bad shit, lots of bad shit, too much just keeps happening. They talk about being "present" and finding balance but let's face it; none of them ever failed at every fucking thing they ever even tried to do. Every one of them had a "big good" happen that balanced all the bad.

I have yet to have my "big good". Now there is some cold, hard, in your face honesty. How's that? Am I a rich, famous writer yet?

Nope.

I had a high moment. When Liz and I married everything seemed to line up. My son had been clean for over two years he was happy with and for us. Liz's son (Erwin was sober, too) came and brought his wife who is an absolute doll. My daughter-in-law even managed to put her bitch on the back burner for the day. Everyone was happy for us... mostly. After a lifetime with a brain like chopped meat I could finally handle any crap that came my way without turning into one huge, raw nerve.

You know... until I couldn't.

See here is what will happen when you finally start to figure out how the Universe works and get your head together. Your brain will decide it is now time for you to deal with *ALL* of the things you stuffed down. It will pull up *every single thing* you have failed to deal with and *order* that you deal with it *right the fuck now* and all at once.

My peace eroded in a sea of the truth in stages, and I couldn't get my peace of mind back because I wasn't used to having it and wasn't really sure where it had come from. But I know just how I lost it, exactly how I did.

Stage one was my ex showing his whole ass over my wearing a tallit, mostly because of what he said and the way he said it. See calling Avy *HIS* grandson like that... It started tearing the tape off the wound.

One of the things I had buried started coming to the surface. One of the many things I had failed to deal with started to rear its ugly head, but... I shoved it back down because having lost my cool I couldn't deal with it. And "stuffing it"... well that was my go-to.

That's what a lifetime of trauma will do. Give you the near super hero ability to relegate even the most horrible things to the dungeon of "That never happened."

When no one ever says *They shouldn't have done that to you...* when no one even tries to help you though trauma... when they in fact *demand* that you think of it as "not that bad" or flat tell you nothing happened... you learn to trust no one—maybe especially yourself.

It had taken me years and lots of hard work to learn to trust myself, but what happened over the next four months would undo everything I had worked so hard for my whole life. You know... any shred of sanity.

Chapter Two

"I just don't think people should do that," I said.

"Why not?" Olivia asked.

"Because it's *not* a baby; it's a dog."

"Some people love their animals like family."

"My son lost a baby; it ruined him and all of us. He couldn't handle it; it's what started first the drinking and then the drugs which probably wouldn't have escalated if he hadn't nearly killed himself on that stupid motor bike driving like an idiot and the doctors put him right on mega doses of Oxy because his back hurt. He had a nice wife—not a crazy psycho one but a nice one who we liked and who mostly liked us. He was looking forward to having a baby; he already loved that baby. Then it was born full term but dead. You could feel the grief radiating from him. He ate it, he breathed it, and he turned to drugs to run from it. It took a chunk out of all of us but nothing like it did to him, and then he and his wife divorced and he's been mostly a mess ever since. He's been clean nearly three years now and he still isn't really himself.

"I've lost dogs that I love; it's not the same. Popping on Facebook and announcing your *baby* just died and you will never be the same and I'm traumatized for them and then... It's a God-damned dog! I love my dog, but when he dies I won't tell anyone my *baby* has died. I have been way too close to losing my son, and he *did* lose a child. People are fucking stupid."

"All people?'

"No, those kinds of people."

"You seem really agitated today."

"Because everything is shitty and then even if I can weave my way through it all I have to deal with the latest stupid thing Trump has done and it's still nearly two months before he takes office. I had hoped that he wasn't really the egotistical all for the rich, racist, sexist he seemed to be. In fact, I'm just going to say it—my greatest hope and my greatest fear was that he just said all that hateful crap to get elected. My greatest hope because then... well we might all be safe."

"And why your greatest fear?"

"Because saying those things got him elected." And *duh* was implied. "That means especially here in the South we are completely surrounded by just the most ignorant, hate-filled people hell bent on taking us back to the day of Jim Crow laws and gays living in the deepest of closets, and women who can't vote."

Olivia looked at her laptop screen. She often does that—stares almost vacantly at her screen. I don't know if she does it on purpose or just because she sometimes finds it hard to look at you when you are really raw. See the only reason I kept going to her after the first visit was because I could tell that she actually cares. They aren't really supposed to, but how stupid is that? I don't think any therapist who doesn't give a damn about their patients could actually ever in a million years help you. Olivia walks with a bad limp. I knew I could work with her immediately because, unlike most college degree wearing people I knew, she understood pain. There is an old Jewish saying, *When you are wounded look for the man who has scars.* Only someone who understands pain can help to heal it.

I have no idea what she is doing—if anything—on her laptop during our sessions because if I stand up she closes it quickly to make sure I don't read anything about myself or anyone else. Therapy is supposed to be private, and believe it or not the fact that she works so hard to protect other people's secrets gives me hope that she will keep mine. See most of the stuff I say in there I would never dare to say anywhere else.

Hell nearly everything I am writing in this I would never say out loud—a lot of it not even to my therapist.

She looks up and catches my eyes and says, "Are you really worried that will happen? That they will start taking our civil rights away?"

"Yes, aren't you? Every really horrible thing that happened to me happened because I was gay. No one wanted me that way—including me. It happened because I was female. Now we have this Orange jackass beating his chest, putting women and minorities and homos down, and all the flaming religious jackals are running behind him as fast as they can fighting over who gets to help carry his train and stand closest to his asshole. The only true thing he said during his whole campaign was that his followers were so loyal to him that if he murdered someone in broad daylight in the middle of the street they would still vote for him. With each leaked possible appointment to his future cabinet it becomes increasingly obvious that he is exactly the person who thinks it's alright for the rich and powerful to grab a woman by her pussy."

"How are you and Liz doing?"

"She annoys the living hell out of me." And I mean it when I say it.

"Why?"

"Because it's always about her. I'm being swallowed in a wave of depression. Everything is going to hell in a hand basket, but if I say anything to her more negative than rainbows and kittens are pouring out of my ass she starts yelling at me, which just makes me wish I never talked to her in the first place. She doesn't care how I feel. She is perfectly happy as long as she just doesn't have to know how I feel. Hardly ever seeing Avy, not knowing where he is or whether he's safe, is killing me. She still sees him almost as much so she's alright and... She has always wanted all my attention. She was jealous of my son and helped put a rift between us. She isn't jealous of Avy; she's crazy about him, but she thinks I should just see him not being there all the time as an excuse for us to spend more time together. But as long as she doesn't understand my pain... I don't want to spend any more time than I have to with her.

"She is just there. She brings home money but she doesn't actually add anything to my life. She is a crappy companion. Her idea of a really great time together is we both sit in the living room and I watch TV while she plays some computer game on her fucking phone and..." I sigh then a great big longing-for-not-what-was-but-what-I-wanted sigh. "I've worked really hard and I've been through so much crap and there ought to be something really great to balance it all out. When Avy was always with us even though it allowed freaking Jenny to run our whole lives at least there was something really good to balance it out."

"I want you to make a list of all the reasons you fell in love with Liz."

It's not just a paper on their wall. Therapists actually learn things in school because you can't make a list like that without remembering that you once had a good relationship with someone. That you were once so in love with them that you risked everything just to be with them.

I was resentful of that list and the first thing I wrote on it was that she was really good in bed which was of course true, but then I started to remember all the things I fell in love with. She used to have the most fantastic smile and a funny smart mouth. She used to be very generous and she used to absolutely dote on me. She was and is beautiful and very smart. Mostly she needed me.

What the hell had happened? Our kids happened, that's what. We tried to blend our families—her fifteen-year-old son, my nine-year-old son, and both of us. At first we pretended we were just roommates, but that didn't last long and then... Well, parents don't want their kids to be gay, and kids sure as hell don't want their parents to be gay. Erwin was already an alcoholic, but Liz just didn't want to hear it much less do anything about it. She has always been really good at pretending there are no problems. Ryan had been trained by his father since he was born to believe that I was an idiot, so the things I wanted for him were all stupid. But the things the much older cooler almost brother wanted... Well, Ryan was all about doing whatever would make Erwin think he was cool. Ryan was in trouble way before I knew what had happened.

If I had to rewrite history there are so many things I would do differently but probably one of the biggest would be I wouldn't have moved me and my son in with Liz and Erwin. Erwin hated me because he was a mostly-drunk surly teenager, very aware of how things looked, who didn't want to have a lesbian mother and of course it was all my fault Liz was a lesbian. Since Levi had already sowed the seeds of "your mother is an idiot to be disrespected and treated like shit" it wasn't at all hard for Erwin to drive a huge wedge between me and my son.

I don't know what might have happened if Liz and I hadn't bought a home together and moved our families together. Maybe we wouldn't have been together at all. Maybe our sons wouldn't have wound up alcoholic and addicts. Maybe things would have been better for everyone and maybe they would have been worse. At the end of the day it doesn't matter at all because you can't change the past. And I was soaking in it and you should never do that when you've had a past like mine.

They say you have to let the past go, but that is hard to do when you are still living with the fallout. Hard to run from the past when it wants to play out in front of you.

And that's what happens when you have PTSD with a big side order of codependency. We all have triggers—

things that pull up unwanted memories—but for a person with PTSD you also get the emotions that went with the memories. That horrible churning feeling in your gut that lets you know you just aren't safe. Forget trying not to see it or feel it because everything that you will try from your whole bag of psychological or spiritual tricks will not work when you start looping. In fact the harder you try not to think or feel it, the worse it will get.

My ex's rants against me after my wedding started cracking the veneer off the things I didn't want to deal with, all the many things I had lied to myself about. I didn't want to admit to the things that happened to me, so I shoved them down, and I shoved them down, and shoved them down.

No one ever wants to admit they were duped.

No one wants to look stupid. Do you know why people get so mad when their mate cheats on them? It's not because unauthorized bodies came together to exchange body fluids, it's because people do it in the first place to prove that they can. To prove the other person is stupid. When someone does something hateful to us, unless we were raised to have a huge amount of self-esteem, our go-to is to find that place where we are the most broken, that agreement we made when we could barely walk that says there is something innately wrong with us, who and what we are. The "wrongness of us" always and forever has every single thing that happens to us be our fault— it's because we are so wrong. No one would treat anyone who wasn't wrong the way we were treated and so… it must be me.

It is not me.

Even if I was stupid or in the wrong place at the wrong time, even if I smiled, or tripped or fell at the wrong time, that doesn't excuse people who happily preyed on my ignorance. In my mind I know that and yet I still can't stop beating myself up. And right in the middle of all this crap… well that was what happened.

Chapter Three

To say I woke up that morning would mean that I actually slept. I came close a couple of times but didn't quite make it. Yet again I was supposed to have Avy, and yet again Jenny found someplace else he just "had" to be at the last minute. She still wasn't taking care of him she had just found other people besides me to do it.

I lay awake most of the night being angry, sad, and resenting the hell out of the fact it wasn't bothering Liz at all. How did I know that? I could hear the bitch snoring even though she was in the other room.

I have heard enough people tell stories similar to mine. For different reasons they wound up raising, or mostly raising, or helping to raise, a grandchild, niece or nephew. Like me they shifted the focus of their life, juggled their schedules, changed what they normally did to accommodate someone else's child. Their lives like mine revolved around the child. The child was used to having them always there, and then the parents decided they were ready to be parents and we're just supposed to stop wanting and caring about the kids so much. You can't just shut that crap off! My heart's broken and at that moment in my life it just felt like everything I'd ever been through was just to cause me pain. I know I'm not the only one going through this same thing, but that doesn't help me. I know some people have it even worse—hell my friend's nephew took his son and moved out of state after she had been raising him for five years. It doesn't make me feel better about what I have lost because it could after all be worse.

There is no balance in my life, no good to combat the bad, and everyone who had ever mistreated me not only didn't get punished for doing so they got rewarded.

I looked at the end of my bed and someone was sitting there. At first I thought it was Liz, and as you might have guessed I was annoyed. But believe it or not I'm not a *shmuck* and just like most of you I vary rarely say what I'm thinking.

I ask, "Is something wrong honey?"

I realize the person sitting on the end of my bed is too thin to be Liz even before she turns to face me and then... I was looking at myself only I was thinner—much thinner—and if possible even more unhappy looking.

In the moment I figure I am having one of those dreams. You know the kind I'm talking about. The ones where you think you are awake but you really aren't and then the things that happen feel that much more real. No such luck. This time I was actually wide awake. I tell myself to wake up and shake myself, and when that doesn't work I jump out of bed, but when I look I'm still sitting there on the end of my bed.

"What the fuck," I say and run my hands down my face and rub my eyes. But I'm still right there.

"Wow, how did I know you were going to say that?" she... or is it I... said.

I do what anyone else in my position would do. I start yelling, "Liz! Liz get in here!"

"Liz is at work. Just a few more months then she retires."

"What the fuck," I say again realizing that I'm right. Now I'm not stupid; I knew this meant my cable had snapped. I try to touch it/me. My hand goes through but I'm still there.

"I'm a ghost, dumbass."

"I'm not dead," I say with conviction.

"Not yet, but you will be if you don't get a handle on your crap. Well actually eventually everything dies, but

20

your time is coming soon if you don't learn to get a handle on your crazy ass shit."

I looked at me. I didn't look much older. I looked rough but not much older. "When do I die, how?"

"Oh I can't tell me that, I'm just here to try to make you realize what you have."

"Crap and garbage that's what I have. God even after I die I'm still going to be a stupid asshole. After the year I've had I'd just as soon be dead, so come on talk to whoever is in charge of such things and snuff my happy ass out right now."

She actually growled at me. "Avy still needs you, Liz needs you, your son needs you he just doesn't know it yet."

"Why don't you go bother them? Tell them they need me and to stop treating me like a bag of dog shit that's on fire on the porch."

"I can't do that. Hell I'm lucky I can do this."

"What are you doing besides proving that I'm completely nuts?"

"I'm here for your reclamation." She smiles. Then I know why. It's a line from *A Christmas Carol* which is one of my favorite movies.

"Then tell me what I should I do and get on with it."

"You have to give up."

Then she was gone and me... well I tried to wake myself up again but... I wasn't asleep.

To say I'd had a bad year would have been an understatement. Shortly after my personal life blew up into a chaotic mess and the Electoral College gave Trump the presidency I hit the very bottom of my personal pit. I figured that had to be what had blown all the circuits in my brain. I didn't for one minute believe that what I had just experienced was real. I asked the Universe at large what I should do and my answer was what? To tell myself that I had to give up.

It couldn't be real. My future dead self couldn't be haunting me. That was just absurd, so it had to be me trying to tell myself what to do but... just give up? I had no idea what that meant, what I was supposed to do with it or what shape it should take in my life. I knew it was something beyond surrender. Everything I was doing, everything I had ever done, had led me to this dark place filled with negative noise masquerading as truths. I was literally talking to myself. I had to give up but give up on what? Everything? Most of everything? Me? In short the message to "give up" didn't really help me.

Obviously I was now to the seeing and hearing things part of the program, so I had lost my battle with insanity and my conclusion at that moment was that if I was going to get sane on any level I was going to have to learn how to give up—whatever the hell that meant.

In the three days that followed I tried desperately to recapture the peace of mind I'd had once and completely lost. At this point my depression had depression. There was no one I could talk to about what I'd seen or heard because I didn't feel like a trip to the ha-ha Hilton was going to help me feel any better. I knew the me I saw sitting on my bed—however I got there—was right. Avy still needed me, Liz needed me, and my son needed me even if he didn't know it.

I tried many things that had worked in the past, and new things people told me about. I was lost and just looking for something—anything—that I could hold onto. Something for me. Something that would be mine but no matter how I flung my hands around in the dark trying to grab anything, I always came up empty.

I was in that place no self-help book or spiritual guru ever really covers adequately; I was completely without hope. I didn't even have enough hope to hope for hope. My spirit was bankrupt.

Giving up was the key to getting a vestige of sanity back. I knew that and yet... I had no idea what "giving up" meant or how to do it.

Chapter Four

It's not Jesus's fault—you know if there ever really was a person Jesus—but his followers... I mean come on, they have caused nothing but trouble. The problem is here in Jakeville in the buckle of the Bible Belt South we're always soaking in it, and these Christians they are NOT about peace and love. Unless you are straight, white, and Christian they really need you to die already and go to hell where you belong so that they can run the world the way it should be.

And let's be honest; a world formed by the Christian right would be hell for the rest of us, and that's what Trump is helping them do to our country. In truth he doesn't believe any of the crap they believe; they are just a means to an end. He is a greedy, power-hungry bastard, and they are easy to use.

As much as we'd like to blame Trump and as much as we can all admit that a fish stinks from the head down, Hitler could have done nothing without the help of the church and its teachings, and Trump would still be just an annoying reality TV star and mega millionaire without them.

The problem isn't with the leaders; the problem is—and always has been—with those that follow wherever their own hate is already leading them. The things "Jesus" taught weren't dangerous. Most of the things he is touted as saying that have real merit had already been said long before by Hillel—all brilliant very spiritual things about love and understanding, giving yourself a break.

So how do we go from that to absolute blind hate? The kind of hate that makes one people rise up and kill another and that fuels the engine of war. The kind of hate that gets someone completely unsuited for the highest office in our land sitting in the White House chipping away at civil rights and chunking the ecology of our planet into a garbage bin for capital gain as he tries to instigate a nuclear war all for the purpose of saying, "I told you so."

How did we suffer through hundreds of religious wars and persecution to get to a time which future generations may call the time of great divisiveness? How do we get from "love people and do what is right" to "those people are different go and kill them"? We got her because religious fanatics believe, and always have, *first* what their leaders tell them and *second* that *only* they are right! Religion splits us firmly into groups. It is written into the very fabric of most religions that if you don't worship God as they do you are an infidel, someone unworthy of heaven and going straight to hell. This has allowed their followers to amass huge armies and kill "other" people in the millions for no other reason than they refused to believe what they believed to be true concerning things that are matters of faith and can NOT be known much less proven.

How can I focus on fixing my own brain as long as that idiot is blowing Twitter up with statements that are fueling the neo-Nazi hate machine? At this time those of us who think and care and feel are petrified and afraid for our planet, our country, our friends, and our families. It seems almost selfish that I am worried about the cracking of my personal brain.

Let me be very honest again. I consider myself to be very Jewish and not religious at all because religion is a bullshit. My mother was born into a Jewish family but they only half-assed practiced. My father was an agnostic. He had been raised Catholic but something happened to him there that made him denounce religion, and let's face it, drove him to be the difficult person he became. He never talked about it nor did members of his family but... none of them were practicing Catholics anymore.

I think it's important to have community, and sometimes the only place I feel safe is in temple on a Friday night surrounded by people who have the same problems I do living in a sea of Fundies. But I don't blindly believe anything. I study *Torah*; I have read *Talmud* and *Mishna* and found many really great things there. I have also read total bullshit there. God isn't a person and he doesn't write books. People write books, fallible, sometimes horrible people. I don't believe everything I read in anything. There are some good stories; some of them teach brilliant things, but I wouldn't argue with someone over whether or not there was an actual Moses.

We wouldn't tell our children the story of "Jack and the Beanstalk" and expect them to believe it was a true story when they were forty.

Look, if I believed "Jack and Beanstalk" was a true story and so I armed myself and went out and started killing anyone over a certain height, society at large would consider me insane, armed and dangerous. They would hunt me down and kill me. My insistence that I read in the Holy book of "Jack and the Beanstalk" that tall people were evil wouldn't save me.

People are never as inauthentic as they are when what they "believe" is contrary to what they know. We get told things are absolute truths when we are very young that no one knows whether they are true or not. In many religions to say "Well that sounds like bullshit" makes you a heretic and so people continue to pretend to believe things long after they know for a fact that it's a bullshit. If faith makes you a worse person instead of a better one what's the point of it? Why are people willing to die and to kill other people over something that can't be proven? How does it help anyone ever to see whole other groups of people as an enemy worth killing over a silly-assed religious belief?

What about all the laws that say things like "treat the stranger as yourself," "take care of the widow and orphan," "don't murder," "don't steal"? I have yet to read *anything* in *anyone's* holy books that says "Don't murder unless you want to," "Don't steal unless you want more stuff," "Screw the widow and the orphan," or "Spend billions of dollars to build a wall to keep out the stranger".

People who think don't attach themselves so firmly to something they don't actually believe. They temper their "faith" with truth and science. They let what they know determine how much they are willing to believe.

Religion is—and always has been—the bully on the playground too big for any one person to stand against.

You would think people would be smart enough not to believe some great orange ape spewing hate, but you see their faith has taught them that people who don't believe exactly what they do are bad, evil and wrong. All the guy had to say was that he was one of them, he hates homos, thinks blacks are uppity, and women need to stick to their place. He's going to do away with such things as saying Happy Holidays—which is inclusive—and make sure we all say Merry Christmas again—even if we aren't Christian. He's going to build a wall and send the Mexicans packing. Shut up all those whining environmentalists who are driving the price of gas up and keeping us from having well-paying jobs.

And all of that—that running commentary in my head—well that was why I wasn't sleeping. I had so many personal problems, so much heartache, and on top of the shit cake of my life a big dollop of Trump.

I told my therapist, Olivia, all that in not so many words. What didn't I tell her was that I had literally had a conversation with my future dead self.

"Alright," she said. She took a deep breath and let it out. I couldn't be sure that it wasn't because of my latest anti-Christian/Trump rant, if she was trying to process my great wisdom, or she was just flat tired. "I can tell you are really frustrated. I think most people are…"

"Not here. Nope. Here most people are putting up their Rebel flags and their Trump in 2020 signs. You know what I want to do…" And I stopped there because well it was yet again one of those things one thinks but doesn't say out loud.

"What's that?"

I thought about it for a second, but then thought that maybe being committed wouldn't be any worse than what was already happening to me.

"I'd love to have the balls to get a shotgun and drive around and blow a hole in every single Confederate flag I see."

"And how would that help?"

"I'd feel better."

"Why?"

"Because maybe—just maybe—they would feel a little bit of the fear they hope to instill in people when they hang them. Maybe they'd get that sick feeling in their gut, maybe they would feel a little less safe."

"So what you want is for someone to feel your pain."

It was more a statement than a question, but I didn't have to think about it.

"Yes I want someone to just once feel as bad as I do. Just once I want someone who causes me pain to feel as bad as I do."

"Can you think of anything short of shooting all their flags that would help you feel better?"

"I have to give up," I said blankly.

I could tell this was the wrong thing to say by the tone of her voice when she asked, "What do you mean?"

"We've already had that talk, Olivia. I don't have the balls to kill myself. I have to give up."

"What do you mean?" she asked again.

"I don't really know exactly what it means. I can't keep fighting all the time. Everything that breaks around our house… when it breaks I have to fix it. I have problems; I'm on my own. Other people have problems; they call me. I just keep trying to feel better about myself and my lot in life, but my life is a crap fest. I haven't seen Avy in three weeks. I talked to him on the phone once for about a minute. He is moving on; he doesn't really want me anymore. I'm lonely."

"Have you started writing again?"

Except for this shit I hadn't written a word in nearly two years. I don't know why she even bothered to ask.

"No."

"Why not?"

"I told you. I don't give a shit about it anymore. It never made me any money. It sure didn't get me any respect, and I see no point in doing it. It's all just lies I put on the page. I'm afraid to write what's in my head and I'm sure no one wants to see it. Nothing at all matters because I don't have my grandson anymore and Donald Trump is the fucking president."

"I think you need to consider writing again. Our time is up. Are you going to hurt anyone?"

"No."

"Are you going to hurt yourself?"

"No."

Why would I hurt myself? Every day is already pain. At night I prayed not to wake up in the morning, and every morning I cursed the Universe that I was still alive.

Chapter Five

A lot of people—not just me—went into a spiritual and emotional decline after the 2016 election. We tried so hard to be above it all and not judge people, but we really can't believe we are surrounded by imbeciles so short sighted that they would allow the country's streams, coastlines, waterways, and air to be destroyed now, to maybe—it hasn't been proven it will—make jobs for the short run.

The very land we sit on is shifting because of all of the fracking that has been going on, but let's lift all restrictions. Let's learn nothing at all from what happened in Flint Michigan and let's just work at nothing so hard as burning a huge hole in the ozone and poisoning the land we live on, the air we breathe, and the water we drink. After all, the world is going to end soon anyway.

That's why the Fundies are dangerous. They want nothing quite as much as they want the world to end so that all the infidels will go to hell and they will inherit the earth.

All this hatred threatens to stomp a Trump-sized hole in human rights. White supremacists are everywhere and feel empowered to be out loud and proud. They mow people down in the street and 45 says, "everyone was wrong." Assailants—many of them ex-military, and all of them crazy—with way too many legal guns keep killing people in mass numbers, but let's neither help our military men be reintroduced to society or help the mentally ill. A God forbid that we should stop either group from buying assault rifles and thirty-round banana clips... Maybe we will do something about bump stocks, but even that hasn't happened as I am writing this, and there was another massacre just last week.

All these religions that believe in the destruction of the world live as if what they believe is true and imminent, and if they don't wake up it will be a self-fulfilling prophesy. They are destroying the planet for the personal gain of the 1 percent; the good never trickles down to us. We get to live in the acid rain they make, drink from the polluted streams, and breathe the noxious air so that they can get filthy rich. They don't have to live in the messes they make. They didn't have to drink the water in Flint.

The corporations could use their billions to create clean energy. But the truth is the filthy rich live above us with water and air filters. To do things right they would have to cut their profit margins, and when forced by regulations to do so do they cut the amount of money they make? No, they pay their workers less or lay them off and make less people do more, and cry about their weak profit margins. No ONE is worth the kind of money they pay themselves.

I'm tired of trying to hang on to something as intangible as my spirituality. I want someone to pay. Maybe I even need them to pay. Someone needs to hold these monsters feet to the fire make them pay to play. They can still be rich, but they need to pay for that privilege instead of making us do it.

How can we NOT judge in this climate? I'm asking mostly because right now I don't know. The people who are struggling the most financially put into the highest office in the land an orange tyrant and gave him the congress and senate which will let him do whatever he wants. A man who is the very picture of greed and avarice is calling all the shots. What on earth do they think he is going to do to make their lives better? Ask one of them and they don't actually have a clue. Their go to is "He will make more jobs." Really? How is he going to do that? By going to war with everyone? By building his stupid-assed wall?

Oh there will be more jobs alright, and all of them will be working for minimum wage doing the jobs Mexicans do now. Here's an idea... How about we don't build a wall. Why are people coming here from South America and Mexico? Because they can't survive there. The political climate is violent and they can't support their families. They are trying to make a better life for their families—the same reason all the white folks came here. Let's spend a quarter of the money we would spend on a new wall, go to South America and kick the tyrants' butts.

Don't blame Hispanics for coming here to work. Blame the Popes because none of them will tell their people to wrap their winkies. Blame the corporations for hiring them because Americans can't live on what they are paying these workers.

I can't hold onto to my spirituality right now because my life is a mess and I am completely surrounded by Trumpites. I can't hear one more time about the evils of Hillary. Don't say you are behind him but you aren't a racist, a sexist, or a homophobe. He spews hate every time he talks; were you just not listening? The only person he gives a pass too is Putin... which he has to because without Russian involvement and the stupid-assed, antiquated Electoral College he wouldn't be president at all.

Where the hell does that leave us? They tell us we all need to vote. They tell us every vote counts. But twice now people who weren't competent enough to wipe their own asses without getting into deep shit won because of a system that no longer serves the purpose it was intended to serve.

It certainly doesn't serve the people.

I wasn't in love with Hillary, but I thought she was a good candidate. I didn't think she would get into office and screw us all for the rich. She might have, but I didn't think she would.

There is only one vestige of hope: most people did NOT vote for this jackass. Ninety-million people didn't vote at all. Of those at least half would have run to the polls and voted if they didn't believe the news media when they kept saying Hillary couldn't lose. Trump lost the popular vote by three million. Now no doubt he will spend millions of taxpayer's dollars—yours and mine because he's giving the rich another tax break—to prove that he won the popular vote, too. But the truth is unless you live in the South more people you talk to are worried sick than are dancing a jig.

Of course we live in the fucking South. Before you say "Just move," our families live here. And how would we do that on what money? Liz is getting ready to retire. I have no real income to speak of anymore, anywhere we would like to live... The cost of living is too high. We're stuck here.

Why did he so clearly win in the South? Because of the Fundies. The Klan—who supported him and he welcomed their support—is still huge here. A member of the clan flying a Rebel flag on line went into a church and killed nine people. There was a debate to remove the Rebel flags from state buildings. From that time till now Rebel flags are flying in yards everywhere I look and on cars and trucks. That's not Southern pride it's pure, unadulterated hate. If you were flying a Rebel flag before this then you can maybe argue Southern pride. If you went out and bought one afterwards... Just admit you have a heart filled with hate.

What's to be proud of? The South has more drug abuse, more alcoholism, more high school drop outs, more teen pregnancy, more divorce? A round of applause! Raise the stars and bars! This place officially sucks ass!

I can't be the only one losing my mind.

Where the hell are we supposed to put the knowledge that there is still so much inequality between the sexes and so much racism? All the ugliness that was hidden is now out for us all to see, and frankly it's frightening.

Here is food for thought: a wound unseen goes untreated and an untended wound festers. We can't lie to ourselves anymore that our country doesn't have race problems, or that we live in either a free or safe country. Maybe now we will move towards fixing what is wrong. Maybe it has to get all the way broken to get fixed. Start with strengthening the border—not between us and Mexico, but between church and state—and getting rid of the Electoral College. That would be a good start.

I will be honest. When 45 won I wasn't surprised. I wanted to be, but I really wasn't. The Electoral College is a dinosaur that needs to turn into oil and be burned up in a hybrid car. I tried not to panic. With his cabinet appointments and his first two weeks it became clear he was exactly what he appeared to be, and things have gone from bad to worse ever since. Turns out I was right. He was put—not voted for but put—into office not in spite of but because of all the hate he spewed and continues to spew.

World War II is not ancient history. There are still people alive who fought in it, who were damaged by it. The Germans rounded people up by the millions. They went into people's homes where they lived with their children and their old people. They took them to murder villages and systematically killed them and cremated them in such great numbers that in a dust storm when you inhale on any part of this planet you are breathing their ashes up your nose. That alone should be enough to stop people from hate.

It isn't.

The horror of World War II is where hate and intolerance leads. It's the same place it has always led. Hate and intolerance are often born and bred in the very places we are told will bring us spiritual enlightenment.

In places of worship. The KKK is a Christian terrorist organization. The Nation of Islam is a Muslim terrorist organization. Both are housed in the US.

The KKK has been allowed to fester in the South since the end of the Civil War. While we run around screaming about Isis and treating Muslim American citizens like scum, we might ought to consider getting rid of all hate groups instead of voting for the man endorsed by many of them.

How am I supposed to deal with my personal problems with all that in my head? Am I just supposed to turn off my brain, my conscience? Should I be as complacent as everyone else seems to be? Is that what I'm supposed to give up on, the hope that the world can ever be a good and healthy place that people can ever stop causing just the worst grief for other people, that humans will ever become fully evolved?

I vote one-issue politics and have since I left the Republican Party. That's right. I said I used to be a Republican, because of course I was raised to believe they were the right people to vote for. Now I vote for the candidates I think are less likely to lead to a time when me—or my neighbors—will be drug out of our houses—just for being who we are—and shot on our front lawns. Everything else we can live with.

When I didn't see myself for most of a week and didn't talk about it with my therapist I decided it really had just been an odd nightmare. For over a year I had been eating a huge stress sandwich with a side order of angst, and I was getting next to no sleep. Not sleeping I decided was why I had such a weird almost dream.

Of course it's my fucked-up life, so after I slept hard two nights in a row I woke up on the sixth day and there I sat again on the end of my bed.

"Craaap," I hissed.

"Yes, I always was so articulate." She/I laughed.

"What do you want from me?" I went ahead and got out of bed—in part to make sure I was really awake, but mostly because I'd always rather be dealing with something that isn't really there from a standing position.

"I want you not to kill us, that's what I want, and you aren't even trying."

"How about you tell me something good is going to happen? How about you give me a little hope? My life feels meaningless and I am in control of absolutely nothing and especially nothing I really care about. I have no one in my life I can count on, and I no longer trust me."

"Well that's not good."

"I know it's not good, asshole."

"You have to trust yourself."

"How the living fuck am I supposed to trust myself? Everything I have done, every decision I have ever made led me here and... I'm miserable here so now what? I have failed at everything I even remotely gave a shit about the more I cared about something the worse I failed. The changes that are being made aren't of my doing and aren't what I want but I don't have any control so I have to live with whatever others do to me. Fucking celiac means I can't even drown my sorrow in cheap pizza and beer. I'm fifty-seven years old. I am sick to death of trying to see the glass as half full. I'm tired of trying to make the best of a bad situation, and I'm most tired of having the only choices I have in life being bad and worse.

"For one brief shining moment in time I was happy being me. I accepted my place in the universe; I wasn't happy but I was content. My rage was in check. I felt as good as I have ever felt and then something horrible happened just like it always does... always!"

"Give up."

"Honey, are you alright?" Liz said as she stumbled half asleep into my room, and the other me was gone. I looked at the clock and it was three in the morning.

"I'm... I had a nightmare is all. Sorry I woke you."

"You need to talk to your therapist about those."

Because of course she, Liz, doesn't actually want to be bothered with my head problems. She needs me around to do all the stuff she doesn't want to do, to fix stuff when it breaks often because she broke it.

I didn't sleep anymore that night. Visits from me weren't helping at all.

"My nightmares have gotten worse," I told Olivia. I didn't tell her they had grown arms and legs and were talking to me when I was awake. "I think what is making me the most depressed is that I had this shit all figured out and now I can't get back there. I keep trying but I just can't and I no longer look forward to anything. Nothing. I don't care that we never have sex, it used to bother me now I think it matters less to me than it does to her. I don't care about writing, or taking care of the animals or the garden or... anything. I'm just so tired of working for everything and never having what I want. I'm sick of always picking shit with the chickens to make the ends meet. I don't know what happened to me."

"Yes you do," she said quietly.

And I did. I did know exactly when I lost the good happy I had going on.

There was an accident. My son had to be hospitalized, and I wound up having to sit in a hospital waiting room with one of my worst abusers and my tormentor as they just took pot shots at me. I held my shit together and didn't make a scene. I kept reminding myself of all the things I'd learned and knew. How none of the crap they were saying and nothing they had done in the past mattered as long as my son made it through his surgery and lived—which he did.

But I sat there for sixteen hours as Levi hinted at what he'd done to me—he had often done that—he flat told me nothing had happened that it was all in my head and then he would purposely say things just to trigger me.

This time I didn't rise to the occasion. I didn't throw a fit. He kept fucking with me, Jenny kept yelling at me just because she could, and I kept my cool.

That didn't keep me from going codependent crazy. The dam on all the shit I'd buried deep in my head broke. It demanded I deal with all of it right then, but unfortunately things in my life just kept going downhill. Since that time, even with therapy, I haven't been able to put the genie back into the bottle.

Once again an unmentionable tyrant is in control and we are powerless to stop him. And my personal life is despair and disappointment.

I look at Olivia. "Knowing isn't really helping, is it? Every time I stick all the nice things together to make a bundle of good someone comes and kicks it apart. I'm just so tired. How am I supposed to use gratitude as my path to spirituality when there is very little that I am grateful for and nothing I am grateful for that isn't attached to some horror? How can I be grateful when everyone has control over me but I have control over no one but myself? I'm sick to death of swallowing how I feel and what I think, but don't want to be yelled at or bullied because I have an opinion.

"How do I not worry about everything when everything in the world and in my personal life is a wall-eyed mess not of my doing? The things that are my fault—I own them; I can work to fix those. The things that aren't my fault are problems I have to deal with that change how, when and where I go and what I do. How can I stop worrying when I have to process all the things I don't want or need in my life that have been thrown at me? I can't do *nothing* because that's not really an option if you are going to keep living. But when every choice you have made has brought you to a place you don't want to be how in the hell do you trust your own judgement? When you have made choices with a clear intention and everything still went to hell... Where do I go and what do I do?

"I'm in a place where I'm damned if I do and damned if I don't. I don't have any good choices; I have bad and worse. Everyone who wants it gets a free shot at me. They get to make choices that hurt me and then I—not they—have to pay for it. I'm not happy at all with the choices they have made for me, but my choice is to shut up and sit down or die. There is no decision I can make at this point that will mean I actually get to be happy or even content."

"You need to do something that you like just for you," she says.

I am honest again as I say, "I no longer even know what that would look like."

Chapter Six

This is what having someone like Trump in the highest office in the land has done—hateful people feel emboldened to do and say whatever they like while more enlightened people fear even having a casual conversation for fear of causing a riot or finding out that someone they loved or admired is actually hateful. The right wingers in this climate all have what I call Republican Turrets. You'll just be having a normal conversation and all of the sudden they are screaming out the party line bullshit: "It's a baby! They are the job makers! They are going to take our guns!"

My therapist has suggested that I am focused on politics because I don't want to deal with my personal problems. She isn't wrong, but for me the political problem *is* personal. Truth is I probably could have handled it a lot better if my private life didn't go to hell at the exact same time and I wasn't already fighting my PTSD nightmares, but I still would have had trouble with anyone like Trump being in office with so much fire power behind him.

See I don't mind change. If it's the change I want to make I'm all for it, but like everyone else I don't want to be in a spot where I feel helpless to make changes for the better. To have someone else—anyone else—make choices that will cause changes I do not want is crazy-making shit for me. When I am working to ignore all the crappy things in my life and I have finally made a bundle of nice which I can convince myself I am grateful for and happy about, what I most don't need is for someone who hates me to kick it apart and then stomp on it till all my sticks are turned into dust.

And that's what happened right on the heels of the election. Everything I was almost used to started to change on a weekly—sometimes daily—basis. The two people I least want to have any control over my life have managed to grab complete control over the only thing I really care about, the person I devoted my life to, the only person I feel really loves me. I see Avy less and less and every week the rules they make change. There is no getting used to the new normal because it changes from day to day. Liz and I have tried all of Avy's life to be a stabilizing force, but now they have made that nearly impossible, and many times the only thing I can do is back off, stay quiet, and pray—which if I'm honest feels more like doing nothing than nothing all the time.

My working constantly to be the best person I can be... none of that stopped them from doing just exactly whatever hateful thing they wanted to do to me. When Jenny didn't want the chore of being a mother she expected me to drop everything and step up to the plate, and she made stepping up to the plate a nightmare, but I put up with her shit to spend time with Avy. I love him more than anything in the world and being separated from him hurts me to the very core of my being. Now they just need us to get out of their way—and by the way we don't have any rights to tell them otherwise—with a big fat order of "fuck you" on the side.

And maybe that's best for Avy. But even if it's not it doesn't matter because again I have no control. Even if it is better for him, what about me? Am I supposed to be alright with feeling like crap all the time, having what I want fall apart on a sea of "He's not your kid"?

No one likes to be tossed aside. No one likes to change everything in their life to accommodate another person's needs, then be told you are much too involved we are going to take this person away because after all they belong to us. You know... now that Avy is big enough to mostly take care of himself and doesn't need constant supervision, now that he isn't too much in their way and they no longer need me to take care of him. No one likes to be dismissed.

I think the fact that I keep seeing myself means my PTSD is getting worse not better, no doubt because there is a constant cascade of crappy things to deal with. The weather is tearing the planet apart but God forbid we should do a single thing to stop climate change and crazy people just keep shooting the living crap out of people but God forbid we do anything approaching gun control, oh and I have no idea from one minute to the next what role I am going to play in Avy's life.

I never doubt Avy's love. He loves me in the way only a child does. Not in that "I love you but you're going to hell" way that the Christians believe in. Or that "I love you even though you're queer" way my mother and many other people do. Or in that "I love you as long as things work for me" way Liz does. Avy loves me and... I need that.

I love him and I need him and they dangle him like a carrot in front of me and dare me to say anything, anything at all to them that they don't like, so that they can snatch him away. They no longer need me to take care of him so now it's all about using him to torture me to get me back for... well whatever it is they think I've done to them.

I want to leave the past behind me. I do; I really do. But how do I do that when my present absolutely sucks? If your present is good then you get to live in the space of all the bad things in your past bringing you to this good place, right? But what about when your present sucks ass.

The person who abused me the most is still calling the shots. He still gets to do things that affect my life adversely. And this is all my fault because you see the Universe handed him to me when he had ODed and was nearly dead when the neighbor found him. The neighbor called me. I ran home to get him and rushed him to the hospital. The whole time I was driving in my mind I was thinking, *If I drive really slow, if I take a "short cut" that isn't, the prick will die. If he dies I get the life I want without having to do anything. If he's dead I get a free ride.*

But I didn't do it. No, I broke the speed limit and... They were rolling him into the hospital on a gurney when he coded. I saved the fucker. Did he think about that when he was screwing me out of everything I had worked for in the divorce? Does Ryan ever wonder why Levi got everything of material value and all I got was Ryan?

I told Levi I was done; I wanted a divorce. He told me I could leave and take my kid but nothing else. That if I tried to get anything else he'd steal my son and I'd never see him again.

And he would have, too, because he is that big of a bastard.

So I left with a kid and got a half-assed job making a buck an hour over minimum wage. Now my son hates me and loves him so... I should have let the bastard die.

The only way I can stop the continued abuse is to just not care. Not love so much so that it doesn't hurt when people don't love me back.

To quote Tony Robbins, "I have to learn to love more and care less."

Why? Because caring leads to worrying and worrying is more than a waste; it's a problem. Worrying about something bad happening in fact releases the same chemical cocktail into our brain that real trauma does. Unfortunately for people with PTSD the amygdala—the part of your brain that holds your fight and flight response—is covered in scar tissue. It's super human like it was bit by a radioactive spider or has been lifting weights.

What happens when someone who already has saver PTSD is forced to live a life filled with stressors? They turn into me. I can no longer process any form of criticism. I can't talk or think myself out of the deep hole I am in. I loop. I have day mares where unwanted, horrible images pop into my head. God forbid if I start talking to anyone about what is bothering me because I will be unable to stop talking. I will tell myself to shut up, but I won't.

I have in fact reached the limit for depression. The only reason I'm not suicidal is because of what I told Olivia—I lack the conviction to see it all the way through. I feel hopeless and yet somewhere deep inside me there must be a glimmer of hope something that says what if I might kill myself just before things were about to get better. In fact, my brain will tell me that and then just as quickly it will remind me that NOTHING has ever worked out the way I wanted it to.

The Buddha said all desire causes pain. That life is pain and it is only through service that we find contentment. I have lived a life of service: so far only a couple of years of contentment, lots and lots of trauma.

There is a reason why most of the enlightened dudes didn't get married or have kids. Having relationships with people you love takes what is hard and makes it damn near impossible. I have only gotten one relationship in my whole life even close to right—the one I have with Avy.

I don't feel loved by most people who say they love me because no one ever chose me. No one in my whole life ever said, "Hey I know let's do what's right for Brenda." Or conversely, "Let's not do that because that is going to completely screw Brenda up." My whole life I have always been at the bottom of everybody's love list. Except my paternal grandmother's and Avy's—I was always in their top ten—but we moved away from my granny when I was four and I went from seeing her all the time to seeing her once or twice a year if I was lucky, and now they have moved Avy and if I'm lucky I get to see him once or twice a month. If I don't kiss Ryan and Jenny's entire ass they could keep me from seeing him at all, which—this might be hard to believe—but I hate having to kiss *anyone's* ass.

You know who always loves me? Little kids. And I love little kids because they haven't learned how not to love yet. They haven't learned to hate. They are incapable of thinking "I love you but you're going to hell." If they love you they love you and they let you know it in a hundred different ways.

When you are different from most people adults immediately judge you and stick you in a box. They categorize you in their heart and hate it when you try to get out of the box they put you in. You know when you aren't the horrible monster they think you must be.

As adults we want to put everyone in their compartment and make them stay there. It's easy because most people are pretty one dimensional, but people who are more layered are problematic. We need them to be this or that not both and they just aren't.

Kids see through the façade, not just because they love people who love them, they see through the façade because we are less likely to put it on for them. I am the most myself when I'm with kids because they don't care that I'm very different. In fact, they are drawn to me because I know how to play. I am fully present when I am with them and they know instinctively that I would willingly throw myself between them and any danger to save them. That's what kids need to know: that they are loved and that they are protected.

It's what everyone needs to know—we're loved and safe.

Unfortunately, everyone says they want people to be authentic, but in truth most people can't stand authentic people. Why? Because it emphasizes the fact that they themselves aren't real. Being in the company of someone who is truly authentic reminds them that they are one-dimensional, phony-assed people. Plastic people have cut out of themselves the part that doesn't fit to replace it with what society wants them to be, and by God you should, too. My Friend Toni façade who is very wise—said, "They want everyone to be their authentic self... You know except you because you aren't right."

Donald Trump is playing a part and so are his followers. They are pretending to be bad asses because in fact they are afraid of everyone and everything. That's where hate comes from; it is born from and thrives on fear. They are afraid of the poor, the blacks, Hispanics, feminists, and queers, so they are attacking them. Trump is a bully, and what do we know about bullies? They strike first because they are afraid to wait to be attacked. They abuse others because they are afraid—always because they are afraid.

Once for a very short time I lived without fear, it was wonderful. I didn't get to keep that feeling. For whatever reason, God, the Universe, or whatever you want to call the energy that flows through everything and really cares about nothing—maybe It's got that "love more and care less" thing down—didn't let me keep it. No, It decided I had to relive every horrible thing that ever happened to me and once I had the imbalance between all the crap I've been through to land in the crap I have now... It screwed up my yin and yang. There is supposed to be equal parts of black and light, some light in the darkness and some darkness in the light, but in my life I just don't see any real light.

Are there moments of brilliance? Yes, but they are brief and always, always, always the darkness follows. The problem is that the darkness is *so* dark, and right now I don't see even a speck of light in it.

I'm a writer. I would *never* have a character go through all that I have been through and then have the reward be... Well so far 45 isn't pulling us out of our houses and shooting us in the head so that's something. I would never let the lead character continue to get kicked in the head every single time they almost got up. In short, I always let my protagonist win. I always let them get what they want. I always leave them in a good place. And that's the thing—you end the book on a high note. If they were real people bad things would happen to them in the course of their lives, but they'd have that high point.

You know who really enjoys a book with an unhappy ending? Liars... that's who.

Everything great that ever happened in my life was connected to something I hated. Nothing was ever perfect. Nothing was ever exactly what I wanted. Most of the time it was close... not at all. I have had people looking in from the outside say I have an enviable life. We all do that, don't we? We look at other people's lives with a kind of envy. They have the freedom, or the mate, the job, or the money that we want. They have done something huge that no one can deny. Mostly they have the respect we crave, need.

When I was healthy I could see the good things in my life and just disregard the crap they brought into my life. I haven't been mentally healthy for most of my life. I loved my dad. He was physically, emotionally and verbally abusive to me. If I had a dime for every time he told me I was stupid I'd be rich. If you could turn in the tokens of disregard he lavished upon me for self-worth, my confidence would make me shine like a thousand suns. Nothing I ever did was good enough.

When dad was good he was very good, and when he was bad he was horrid. To love someone so much who has nothing but open disdain for you—unless they love you at the moment, which they do in spurts—will completely screw up your idea of love and leave you with no self-love at all. My father was wonderful in so many ways: funny, intelligent, creative. If he had just been one-dimensional, if he had just been an asshole, then eventually I would have walked away from my feelings of being unworthy, of wrongness. But he wasn't. He was an amazing, animated fellow who could charm the birds out of the tress... until the darkness washed that away and he blew completely up and took it out on his whipping boy. Unfortunately, I was that whipping boy.

But the worst was yet to come. At sixteen he married me off to a thirty-four-year-old man in order to keep me from being queer. Honestly, I wanted to marry him. I thought it was a good idea. Why did I talk myself into the idea that I loved this man, that I wanted to get married? Because three months before that my Dad took one look at the way I was dressed, flew into a rage, and beat the living crap out of me for thirty minutes screaming over and over that he wasn't raising a fucking dyke.

Marrying that man was not a good idea, and the abuse he heaped on me was worse for my soul than anything I could have ever imagined. I had traded one kind of abuse for another, and I hadn't traded up. My father had at least loved me. Levi was a textbook narcissist incapable of loving anyone but himself. A pervert who enjoyed nothing quite as much as making people want to blow their own brains out. He was a master manipulator and a crook who used people and threw them away like toilet paper.

When the father you love signs you away to a monster because of the wrongness of you, it's hard to find any self-worth. Why did I stay with him so long after the drugging and the rape? Because my father was old school all the way and women who got used the way I had been used were asking for it. And it happened because I was stupid. See, Levi had bragged to me already that he had done similar things to both of his ex-wives. And who did I blame? Them. So when it was me... well it was my fault. I should have known he couldn't be trusted, after all he had told me who he was. He just kept telling me it was all in my head. Though I never could rationalize the fact that everything in my pants hurt I didn't want it to have happened so I also kept telling myself it didn't and it was easy to do because since I had been drugged out of my gourd when they did it all I really had was nightmarish shadows. I stayed with him because I knew if I didn't my father would not let me come home, that he would blame me, that I would be on my own. My mother... well since my younger sister Fran was born—eighteen months after me—I had never really existed for her. She loved me but had never had my back. Dad's been dead for over ten years now, and still when she talks about him it is only the good stuff. She wouldn't have said anything against what he wanted because she never had.

If you claw yourself out of a lifetime of abuse in a world that doesn't want you and convince yourself you have worth and become content with your lot in life and then the Universe arbitrarily takes it away from you, you have nothing left. I was reliving over and over every horror I had ever buried under a thick layer of lies to protect myself. Every time I had nearly dug myself out there was another horrible thing to deal with. By the time the orange ass hat won the election and then my family imploded and there was nothing I could do to stop them from doing just what they did, I not only had nothing left but had eaten into the reserves.

I knew seeing and talking to my future dead self meant I was crazy because it couldn't be real.

What kind of God would expect me to once again climb out of a foaming pit of bile with no promise of better on the other side? I keep crawling out and things keep being as bad or worse than what I just crawled out of. I don't know that I have what it takes to do it again. I keep crawling out and getting through and nothing I ever do is good enough. I have never really had any control over my own life and the people that did all seemed to be hell bent on destroying me.

Every driving force in me was to get successful enough that no one could hurt me anymore and... I never had time to succeed because I was way too busy just trying to survive whatever bullshit the Universe decided to shit on my head that day.

I was tired of even trying, and what did the people around me do? Distance themselves from me. My friends all got too busy to even call, and Liz spent more and more time on her phone playing games.

See I was usually really good at masking my depression—as we know humor is born in a sea of pain and so I was supper funny, vivacious, outgoing. I was normally the life of the party because at least when people were engaging with me, laughing at me, I felt wanted. I was so depressed I couldn't just pull happy right out of my ass for them and so the same people who always came to me to whine every time they got a fart turned crosswise abandoned me like flies leaving a corpse when the stink is gone.

And I stopped going anywhere or doing anything. I stopped going to temple. My theater group asked me to take a part in a play; I turned them down. Yes I was doing that same thing I had warned friends not to do hundreds of times. I was depressed and so I was just steering clear of anything that might drag me out of my depression because I just no longer felt like putting on an act. And no one, not one person reached out because I was their "go to when they were depressed guy" and none of them could even begin to deal with the fact that I was losing my shit.

I couldn't care enough to even try to pull myself out of the pit. I needed help, and what did the Universe do? It sent me to tell me to give up.

I had been working my ass off all day on the place because that's what I do when I can't cope with my life, I work myself into a comma.

Did I tell you that I have a small farm? Well I do. It's a hell of a lot of work, and I had just learned that yet again a giant turd had landed on my farm and not in the garden where it might have done some good. I was physically beat and lower than dog shit. Here's a truth; doing something that fails abysmally will take as much if not more work than something that works. When something works you at least have a moment of satisfaction, but when it doesn't...

Liz was working late. I went in and started dinner because I almost always do all the cooking.

I had just washed my hands and started to get in the refrigerator wishing I had thought about what I was going to make for dinner a lot earlier in the day when a voice said in my ear. "Just give up!" I jumped and turned around to face myself because you see trying to numb myself out with work hadn't really worked and I'd been thinking about it all day.

"Why are you... am *I* so thin? Do I have cancer?" I demanded of my future dead self.

"Nothing that dramatic." She laughed, and I remembered that I used to have a really good sense of humor. The last year had flat beaten that out of me. "Just give up."

"What exactly do you mean *give up*? On what, on who?"

"Just give up."

"That's really not helping."

Then she was gone.

What now? What the hell was I supposed to do? Nothing? I supposed to do nothing, was that the answer? I wanted to get back to where I once was in that contented space. But how? I'd done everything I could think of to try to claw my way out of the pit and so far every time I almost got there someone kicked me in the head and I slid all the way back to the bottom. Did giving up mean I should do what I was already doing and not even try to get out of the pit? Just stay there and get comfortable in the negative space?

Why did I tell me to give up today of all days?

One of the things I raise and have always raised is goats. A few years ago dogs got in and killed everything I had. Then the most amazing thing happened. My friends raised the money and bought me all new goats. That's wonderful, right? In fact, I'm just going to say that act of absolute kindness and love from not a couple of people but from literally dozens was one of the things that made me think I just might be worth a shit after all. It's still amazing that they did that, but—in my life there is always a but—I hate it but there you have it, another but.

About two years ago one of the goats developed a swelling on her knee. I figured it was an injury. Then one of the kids started stumbling till it couldn't walk. I took the goats to be tested. The vet took blood. I waited. It turned out it was exactly what I was afraid it was—CAE (Caprine Arthritis Encephalitis)—they get it from their mother's milk. It is horrible and debilitating. Some goats carry it and have no symptoms, but others die soon after birth. The only thing you can do is breed them, take the kids as soon as they drop and feed them milk replacer. Last year I got exactly one doe kid and so I had to breed them again. She was dry when I found her, but her brother was still wet and I thought *she's got to be clean right, right?*

This spring she kidded while I was out of town and so her kid nursed. Since I thought she was CAE free I wasn't really worried… till the kid started stumbling. So I took her mother to get tested and of course she tested positive which means her kid has it, but the kid got better. (The other kid that got sick had to be put down, and yes I had to put her down. Hey I told you my life is crappy!) But it doesn't matter because now I have to get rid of her and the kid plus the two old does after they kid. Maybe they will have does this year and maybe they won't, but I can't breed them again. Even if I get to their kids in time I will still have to wait for six months to have them tested (you know because my life needs to suck at all times or the Universe feels cheated!). If those could-be kids are CAE free I will still have a herd; if not I have some major decisions to make.

Is that what I should give up on? Is that what I mean when I tell me to give up? Get rid of all the goats; don't get new ones. Maybe stop farming altogether... and do what exactly? I hardly get to see Avy; I no longer have him to take care of. My career is completely dead. The farm is actually the only thing I do that brings in steady money/food. I sell a little milk, I sell some eggs, I garden we eat. These days I make nearly as much off the farm as I do on my books, so as I said before my career is dead.

But I'm not bitter about life!

Here's something else people don't say out loud. God doesn't care. Most days I still believe in God, not all but most. But I don't think God actually cares about any of us—at least not the way we care about things. If God cared, bad things wouldn't happen. The Holocaust wouldn't have happened. Climate change wouldn't happen. Good people would have good lives and bad people would have crappy ones or just die and get out of everyone else's way. Looking at the evidence: God, the Universal Energy, or whatever you want to call it, is either sadistic or most likely is transcendent as it says in the Amidah. God—according to Jewish belief—is outside human understanding and so doesn't think or feel like we do.

God isn't in control.

That's what makes sense—that God doesn't have control. If we have free will bad things happen to us because our free will smacks into the free will of an asshole. So God has figured out the "loving without caring" thing. God therefore loves us but doesn't care what happens to us—which is obviously true but not particularly comforting. Many religions rush to give God a face and human emotions to make God more approachable, but that sort of belief means that when bad things happen to us it must be our fault—which is the seat of shame.

Shame sucks. The love without caring doesn't really make our lives better, does it?

People have a need to slap a human face and emotions on God. They want a divine being that they can reason with, someone who cares.

There is NO proof that such a God exists. Look, why do some people thrive on this planet, some get by, and some have lives they make into a living hell? That's right I am making my life a living hell. Sure, I'm having a lot of help, but a lot of what is wrong with me is my perspective... at least that's what I've learned from that mountain of self-help books I've read that were all written by very successful people with balanced lives.

I know that one of my biggest problems is that I'm a fixer. One of the things I can't seem to let go of is the notion that I ought to be able to *do something* that would actually *fix* something... *anything*... in my life and make it good. I ought to be able to help my friends, family, and the world be happy.

I can't.

I know from experience that everything I try will only make things worse or at best keep us all alive to get by another day so that we can deal with another river of cascading caca. There will be no payoff for the work, the pain, the frustration which is my life.

That's one of the biggest problems I'm having right now: I know what's wrong; I just can't fix it.

I did have it all figured out and I knew that being worried and angry all the time can only make things worse not better. I knew I should be impeccable with my words, know my intentions, not take things personally, not make assumptions, always do my best and not to be concerned with the out-come, have no desires. I know I should change the things I can and let go of what I can't and just make the most of what I have. That love is the answer and all that other flowery bullshit, but knowing all of that doesn't change the awful way I feel right now in the present—which is supposed to be the only place I live. It doesn't kick self-doubt out of my head. I'm unhappy; my life is a mess; there is no candy-coating it.

How can I not worry about the next shoe dropping when the past tells me that if I relax and just try to enjoy the things that are good in my life right now someone will come and hit me right upside the head with that shoe or—you know—a fucking baseball bat.

When I worked my ass off and spent a couple of hundred dollars on formula bottle feeding a goat trying to get a new herd... She still tested positive. A horrible thing happened, my amazing friends busted their asses to help me in my time of need and despair and... they brought me CAE infected goats. Which, if I'm honest, is more heartbreaking then walking out and finding my whole herd ripped apart by other people's "fur babies." God, that term puts my teeth on edge.

If CAE isn't the Universe giving me a big fat *fuck you*, you tell me what is.

Maybe *that's* my problem; I take everything personally. If God doesn't care enough to help me and give me a good life why would God go out of God's way to rain shit on my head? It's just life, right?

It doesn't feel like it's "just life". It feels like the plan is to make me as miserable as is humanly possible. Other people's "just life" isn't filled with death and dismemberment—all bad things. Some people get exactly what they want.

I should trust. I sometimes think the entire human experience is only to teach us trust but... Why? What good does it do to trust? Trust in what? That things will get better? They will; they will get slightly better and then just when I start to relax everything will go to hell in a handbasket. Trusting God doesn't matter because God may love us but God doesn't care. He isn't going to come to my rescue or He already would have dozens of times. If God cared and ran the show, the world would be an amazing place filled with kids that never got sick, all got a bike and a pony, and grew into people who got everything they ever wanted.

We have free will. Without free will there would be no point to this life. But our free will means everyone else has it, too. Since God doesn't actually give a crap about us He isn't going to save us any more than He has saved anyone else. Read your history books, people. The worst people—the rich, the greedy, and the power mad—have always been able to destroy the lives of everyone else.

To think that God saves one undeserving piece of crap from a life of drugs and crime because he prayed for deliverance but allows a good person to be stomped to death for being in the wrong place at the wrong time doesn't make any sense.

If we believe God cares, then I for one will fall into a shame spiral which leads to the darkest corner of never-good-enough. Because if God cares for me, where is the proof? My life tells me God doesn't care about me; that even though I pray every day God's not listening. If that is the case, what makes me so unworthy? I know that the only reason for prayer is to remind myself to try to do better, to take heart, to listen when the Universe speaks inside me.

The Universe hasn't spoken inside me in a long time; no, it sends a manifestation of my future self to tell me to give up. Which, frankly, is making things worse not better.

Trump is the fucking President of the United States. He is currently doing everything in his power to destroy this country for everyone but the top one percent. He gave his rich buddies another tax cut "five" to go with the "one" Bush gave them—which caused our last major recession. They got a huge tax cut; we got *bupkus*. Am I worse than Trump? Worse than the greedy rich? They have everything they want and their life is made easy by having huge amounts of money they hoard.

How do I find my way back when that is what my brain does to me? Put a magnifying glass on all that is wrong but it can't find anything good. Not right now.

Chapter Seven

"Do you know why there is a bed bug epidemic in this God forsaken country?" I ask Olivia.

She has been sitting very ridged and trying not to act like I might have them with me ever since I told her I found the fucking things in my God-damned house, and I am not judging her at all because that's how freaked out I am by them.

"All my clothes have been washed and dried on high heat and I now keep them in sealed plastic bags on the table in the dining room. I take my pajamas off when I get out of bed and bundle them with the bed linens, take them right to the washer and stick them in. I take a shower, wash and blow-dry my hair, and then I dress in the dining room, and my skin still crawls all fucking day long."

"Why do you think we have a bed bug epidemic?"

"Because it is shameful to have them; that's why. There are no ads on TV. You know the fucking things are everywhere because there is an entire wall of product at the hardware store, but no one ever tells you they have them."

"Why do you feel ashamed?"

"My house is full of bed bugs."

"I thought you said they were only in your room."

"We don't know that. You can never know that. They can hide anywhere. I have burned most of what was in my room—a lot of it stuff I cared about, that I loved. My mattress and every other mattress in the house is in a bug-proof sleeve. I burned all the pillows in the whole house, bought new ones and put them in sleeves. I sprayed some stuff called Cyonara that I accidently got on my arm and it blistered my skin. (Not surprising. It's not called "goodbye" for nothing.) I bombed the whole house. I sprayed the whole house. I get up and check my bed three and four times a night, but I still have them. Just a couple and they're sluggish, but... I'm exhausted. I'm not really sleeping. I'm up by five—and I already told you how I start every day and then I start spraying and burning stuff again."

"Have you thought about hiring an exterminator?"

"The exterminator wants $300.00 a room, you still have to do all the cleaning and moving of furniture because he doesn't, and he will only guarantee it for three months."

"It may be worth it."

"I don't have that kind of money and three months isn't going to cut it because they can lay dormant for up to a year. I am doing everything in my power to make sure I don't take the damn things with me when I leave my fucking house."

"You said you spray the house naked?"

"Well I don't want that crap on my clothes or to take my clothes into the bug room."

"So when the spray blistered you..."

"Yeah. All over. I hardly get to see Avy as it is and now I'm thinking it's a good thing because I don't want to bring him into the bug house. I don't dare let Jenny get wind of the fact I have them—though in all honesty how do I know I didn't get them from them in the first place?"

"You don't. You don't know who brought them into your home but... why are you ashamed? You didn't put bugs in your house, and you are doing everything in your power to get rid of them and to make sure they don't spread from your house to others."

"You know what? You're right. Why should I be ashamed? The mother fuckers are taking over the country; it's not my fault. Fleas are worse. I mean they literally carry the plague! People get those in their house all the time and they don't hide that they have them. No one is ashamed to say they got bitten by a fucking mosquito; they drink your fucking blood, too, and talk about carrying disease. Bed bugs don't carry disease. Hell lots of people don't even have a reaction to their bite..." So I almost talked myself out of it, but... "...I feel filthy and ashamed, deeply ashamed."

"But it isn't your fault."

"They are in my room."

"But you have already said you spray your luggage when you go away. You wash all your clothes as soon as you come home, and you don't keep your luggage in your bed room. You had a big party and friends put their coats and bags on the bed in your room. Your wife works for a public college. You said she keeps her purse and her coat in your room. Someone brought them into your room; you are dealing with it; it takes time to get rid of them. I don't think you should be spraying toxic chemicals without protective clothing I think you need to stop burning everything you own. I think you need to actually sleep."

Was Olivia right? I knew she was. But I kept spraying naked and burning shit and not sleeping for six months till my insanity had reached an all-time high and there wasn't a single bug of any kind living in or around my house.

And that was a flashback to explain why the goat that just tested positive didn't get tested before I bred her. See the time when I need to have her tested happened right in the big middle of the bugpocolypse. When I wasn't thinking and was basically just sort of running on vapors and Cyonara.

The bugs had turned my home from a safe space into the last place on Earth I wanted to be. I stopped inviting people into our home. I spent nearly all day every day outside to stop from going in. When it got dark I dreaded it. I felt like the Universe had stripped me of everything that gave me comfort. The Celiac had stripped me of my comfort foods—of course I immediately replaced those with candy and sweet crap so I didn't in fact lose any weight I gained it eating stuff that never tasted the least bit satisfying. I was stuck drinking wine.

The worse things got the more I tried to be more spiritual. There were a lot of reasons for that. Most people who do it do it to buy hope, but if I'm honest I do it for a different reason. The more my life sucks the more I need to know why we are even here and why my life sucks. Did I make a huge karmic debt in my last life that can only be paid by always having difficult people in my life who make me their whipping boy? You know: giving my goats the plague, filling my house with bugs, giving me a disease that strips pleasure from my life.

Does it bring balance to my soul that I'm suffering? No it makes me bitter and angry, makes me feel worthless. Hardship is not *growing* my soul it is *depleting* it, so a spiritual path... well it's also a bullshit.

Spiritual gurus promise that we can end our suffering by focusing on gratitude, letting go of our pain, and moving to a place of peace through meditation and prayer, *namaste* and all that good crap. Maybe if your head isn't a complete mess and people don't walk by and slap you upside the head as you try to find peace and balance your energy, this might work. This is not the world I live in. I live in a world filled with difficult people who love to make me suffer; it empowers them. Or I have people in my life who make huge messes then expect me to fix it. Mostly they made huge messes then walked away leaving me to either try to fix them or live in the hole they left behind.

Here is the big problem with that. I can't fix problems other people make once they make them. At best all I can do is repair part of the damage. So what happens to me because of these difficult people? I have gotten to a point where I walk around carrying, and sleep beside, a big bucket of putty—just in case in the night the dam begins to crack in the hope I can fix it before it has a chance to break. I do this in an effort to find peace because when someone is constantly blowing holes in your life there is no peace, but I think if I am prepared I can get some peace for myself.

Just a little peace of mind—it shouldn't be too much to ask for. But it always is when we have difficult people in our lives because they just want to do what they want to do. If you love them you'll clean up after them, pull them out of a pool of their own vomit, and never tell another living soul how bad you feel. You'll help them keep all their problems a secret—you know so that they can make other people's lives suck as much as they do yours.

You'll lie by omission the way you do when you have bed bugs—and for the same reason. It isn't your fault but it feels like it is, and there is a shame attached to it that makes it hard for you to talk about it. All you can do is do everything you know how to do and hope the problem goes away.

Just give up. What does it mean? What does it apply to?

Maybe I should give up on this friggin' country. Trump and his army of Bible thumping, Rebel flag waving bigots have won. We can't really take it back from them because our vote doesn't count. What can we peons do to change anything?

No one has been able to stop him yet. Russian collusion rolled off of him like water off a duck's back. People just keep shooting and killing whole groups of people. Most of them are his supporters. He just keeps saying stupid-assed, unhelpful, even hurtful things. When he does his supporters cheer. As long as they aren't the ones getting shot they don't care.

People like Trump and his followers are psychic vampires; they eat the energy of everyone around them.

They are soul-sucking leaches, and the energy they love to consume the most is fear.

Spiritual leaders will tell you to pluck the toxic people from your life, but that is hard to do when the country you live in is being run by them and even harder if it is someone you love—especially your kid.

How do I go from bitching about Trump to my kid? I thought it was clear. As I am writing this I am as crazy as a shit-house rat! This is what my brain is doing right now. It is bouncing from one awful thought to another like a ball in a pinball machine. It doesn't have to make sense. Nothing I have ever written has ever made me enough money to actually pay the bills, and this fucker will never see the light of a printer much less publication, so... I'll do what I want! Don't give me a lecture on syntax.

My kid drills a huge hole in my life, makes me wish I was dead, and then I'm the bad guy. That's right; I'm the villain in his story because after all I just keep running around getting in his way as he is trying so hard to punch a giant hole in the dam. He has a sledge hammer smacking away and why can't I just get the fuck out of the way and let him do what he wants to do and stop putting putty in every crack he makes because after all the dam is going to break anyway and when it does that will be my fault, too!

Try, just *try* to stay deeply spiritual when you are standing with your grown child in the emergency room for the second or third time because they have ODed. Remain deeply centered as you go to visit them in jail. Be filled with gratitude that at least this time they only totaled the car and didn't kill themselves or someone else as you listen to the therapist in his rehab call you an enabler.

Pretending that you have it all together and are still spiritually healthy—well that is the codependent's super power—right up until it isn't.

You can only pretend just so long. Only hide the truth from yourself and everyone else for so long. Then the truth of the hole they have dug in your life becomes a blinking neon beacon saying, "Here's the dumbass with the Kick Me sign on her back, take a whack." I ran out of putty, the dam broke, and I'm ass deep in a mess I didn't make but that I take full responsibility for because after all it was my job alone to make sure the shit didn't hit the fan.

People are the most inauthentic when what they "believe" is contrary to what they "know." What do I mean? Think about it for a minute. A belief is often something we are taught we are not to question—a matter of faith. When we know certain things but cover and hide them under a "belief" we can't be authentic. The person who is secretly gay but suppresses it because of their "belief" that all gay people are evil cannot be authentic. Somewhere they know it isn't a choice and it isn't wrong, but they are afraid to let go of their "belief." They are afraid they will be punished for their "sin."

I can scream to the top of my lungs that everything is alright, but if it isn't, it isn't. Pretending that I still have my spiritual mojo as I am baling water out of the living room floor of my life means what I believe is contrary to what I know. Everything is not alright and it isn't going to be unless something changes and... It's a total bullshit that you can always be the change you want to see because sometimes the change you want to see is for your loved one get their fucking act together, and you have *zero* control over that.

Here's a truth that isn't a bullshit: you will never do evil as long as you actually follow your heart—not your ego but your heart. But following your heart is not a guarantee to happiness or even contentment. Nope, sometimes following your heart will absolutely take you to a place where you will find the most pain.

Life is a fucking poker game and some of us get dealt a really bad hand over and over and over again.

A man who has a best friend that is Hispanic but voted for the guy who wants to build a wall may "believe" there needs to be a wall because it's what his party believes, but he knows good and well there does not need to be a wall. That repressing other people will not make him rise. That boundaries of any kind are actually fences for everyone and are completely arbitrary.

No one except the rich are repressing anyone. No one but the rich can. If they don't want the minimum wage job pulling cabbages they need to shut the fuck up!

Success is dumb luck—all just dumb luck! I know people who haven't made it who are just as talented and have worked twice as hard for the same dream as other people I know who made it. The people who made it in most cases are not nearly as worthy as the people who didn't; they didn't pay as much dues. For every winner there is a loser and often the loser worked harder and did better—and lost anyway.

There is a rich man in the White House who stole an election. He cheated to get in. He stole a position of ultimate power. Levi is the scum under pond scum. He was always happy. He was always richly rewarded for being a douche bag. So what is the obvious conclusion? That the only way to succeed is to be a lying, cheating, weasel.

Where is the fucking balance? Those of us who fail over and over and over again but just keep going even though no one cares what we do, are we to be commended or do the words "That poor simple fool" apply to us? Where is the peace?

At this very moment I'm about as low as I can get. People are making changes that maybe they need to make that impact me in many negative ways. I have no control; I just have to live with their decisions. The car broke down twice in the last two months costing nearly eight hundred dollars. The dryer finally died—after years of me putting it back together and keeping it going with bubble gum and spit—that was four hundred. The truck had issues. At least I could work on it, but parts for it were two hundred. I was super depressed and didn't get any firewood because my saw needed to go to the shop and... well everything else was breaking.

A guy I have done stuff for free for over and over again was supposed to sell me his odds and end pieces—weird-sized pieces that won't work in a commercial rick of wood—for thirty dollars a rick, but he changed his mind and wanted fifty. At that price it's cheaper to burn natural gas, but we can't really afford that either. I put my saw in the shop. I put it in the shop because I couldn't fix it. It was there for six weeks because they had to order a part that cost a hundred and fifty dollars.

The goats are sick. After nine months I still don't sleep without getting up numerous times and looking for bugs. My writing and the farm barely break even so we are living on Liz's teacher's salary. Now I guess I should be happy that I could pay all those bills and now I have a saw that runs and cars that run so we can get where we need to go—and now I can cut firewood.

That's the up side, right? The silver lining.

And that's the problem right there. Horrible things are happening for me, things I hate. We are seriously low on cash—after taking one hit after another—right before the holidays. And I'm supposed to pull contentment from the fact I could actually pay all those bills and now I can cut firewood?

Really, that's supposed to make balance? Let's face it; no one wants to be in a position where they have to bust ass to cut wood because otherwise they can't afford to heat their house.

That's not balance, mother fuckers! A pretty sunrise or set, a rainbow and a nice tree bundled with those things isn't going to balance out a huge negative. It just can't. I am trying—I really am—to bundle the nice into a big enough pile to balance the double or triple negatives in my life, but I just can't do it. Having a huge orange bastard in the White House making sure that none of us really feel safe... Well it's not helping any more than being haunted by my future dead self is.

It's a good time to be part of the one percent and a bad time to be anyone else, so... Where am I supposed to put all that? There isn't room in my brain or my heart for all this shit.

I never know what is going to set me off when I am dwelling in the bottom of the pit. I just heard Garth Brooks sing his song about unanswered prayers and how happy he is for them. It is so easy for people who have everything they could every want need or desire to say such things. His assumption that God cares only proves that he doesn't understand the nature of God at all. The people who are given their heart's desires are no more deserving than those who aren't. In fact I'm just going to say they aren't.

Pick any big-named actor, writer or artist, and there are people who are better who will never make a dime—not a dime. Hundreds of actors, writers or artists could live on what one of them makes, but there is nothing for the rest of us, nothing is left over—nothing. Why does one person achieve so much while others do the same work to achieve nothing?

It is NOT because of hard work or perseverance. No one in the writing industry is any better than I am (ego about your work is sometimes all you have) certainly they have not worked any harder than I have. I dare say that most of them would have given up way before I did if they had failed as many times as I have.

I was at a signing once and next to me was one of the heavy hitters of the SF world. I had no line at all (I signed five books the whole hour); she had a line out the door.

I said jokingly pointing at the line, "I can help you with that if you need."

She looks at me smiles and says, "You have to pay your dues, kid."

She is a nice gal and just clueless so I just spiral into a depression and don't say a word of what I'm thinking which was this: *Really, bitch? Because I know your story but you don't know mine. Mommy and daddy gave you a top-notch college education. You decided you wanted to be a writer and because of the education you were given you got a ten-thousand dollar grant to write a book. I have never been handed anything and I have written more books than you have, so who didn't pay their dues?*

Give up. Didn't I do that already? I don't write anymore. I don't expect anything good will ever happen for me anymore. If giving up is the answer, why am I not already fixed?

I'm sick to death of hearing the rich blaming people for being horrible failures. Stop telling us it is our fault! If I had worked half as hard and succeeded they would hold me up as an example of bravery, courage and wisdom. It isn't my fault if I have busted my ass and tried and tried and tried and never won at anything.

It would be different if I had sat on my ass and expected riches and fame to fall on my head. If I expected that success would find me without work and failure then blamed the Universe because I didn't have what I wanted in life. If I didn't constantly work at fixing my head or trying to align my soul with my personality or make choices with a clear intention. If I never tried meditation or didn't work at committing acts of love and kindness; if I wasn't kind or compassionate; if I wasn't working on being the best me I can be—then someone could say I hadn't paid my dues. Hell I feel like I've paid mine and everyone else's. Meanwhile I'm sitting at a deficit.

Some people whine their way through life instead of fighting the good fight. They frankly deserve whatever happens to them because they aren't even trying.

But you know what? I am trying. I make myself get up every morning and do the best I can. I work my ass off. I do my best not to make a hole in the ozone or other people's lives. I don't pollute the world. I am kind to people. I help people when I can. I pray, I go to therapy, I do *che gung*, I try to meditate. In short, I am doing everything I know how to do to try to find some peace of mind some contentment. I reached that moment once, and the Universe jerked it away from me.

Why? Why can't I have what I want? Nothing I want for myself would hurt anyone else. If I can't have what I want, or even *need*, how about just some piece of mind? A good night's sleep—I'd settle for that. How about I can have a pizza and a beer without being sick for weeks. How would it destroy the world as we know it if I were to win at anything at all?

And all that was in my head the whole time I was cooking dinner. I can't tell you what I cooked, but I can tell you what it tasted like—defeat.

The next time I showed up it was at the foot of my bed in the middle of the night again. I rolled onto my back and flipped on the light.

"At least help me look for bugs."

"There are no bugs, head case. The fact you and Liz don't both glow from all the chemicals you drenched this house in is a small miracle. Just give up."

I put my hands over my ears. "Stop saying that! Just tell me what the fuck you mean and go away or just go away but stop saying that, you fucking asshole."

"One of your biggest problems is the way you talk to and have always talked to us."

"Christ, are you trying to be my therapist now?"

"Well you spent so much time there I learned a lot."

"I only go once every two weeks."

"Yeah, that's going to change."

"Just tell me what you want me to do. Ghosts always suck in stories; it's always the same; they show up and say parts of things. I mean for the love of God just say what you fucking mean and... what the fuck kind of ghost are you anyway? I'm dead in the future. Only I could get haunted by my own ghost."

"Everyone is haunted by their own ghosts. Give up."

"God dammit leave me the fuck alone!"

"Sorry can't do that. You're going to kill me."

She left just as Liz came running into the room, "Are you..."

"I'm fine. I just had another nightmare."

"I think... you should go to therapy more often."

"Yeah." I didn't even try to argue with her. After all, wasn't that what I had just said?

I never got back to sleep, and future me should have known that screwing up my sleep wasn't helping me with the whole sanity thing.

If the Universe doesn't want to give me anything else that's fine, but give me back the coping skills it took me a lifetime to learn that it only took one day to unlearn.

Chapter Eight

The problem is always in that space where someone else's free will bumps heads with yours and their balls are bigger than yours. They get exactly what they want and you don't. They use you and you are just used. They abuse you and you are just abused. Expecting that they will be sorry for how they hurt you, that someday they will understand, or pay or anything else. That is the place where they broke you and you can't get past it.

We are supposed to pursue justice but sometimes there will be NO justice at all. This is the space so many of us entered the minute they announced Trump had won the election. Everything he has done since has just made us feel more screwed by our country and by life. When they gave the richest people in the country a tax cut by raising taxes for the middle class, Trump told us it was a Christmas present for us. Yes and here's a giant jar of Vaseline to go with it. He is destroying our way of life. We are helpless; we should consider ourselves blessed.

Here is the worst part: the people who supported him—the ones who put him in office—they also didn't get a tax cut and most of the government aid that they need to survive is going to get cut. Do you know who they will blame? The homos, the Mexicans and the blacks—they don't call us anything that nice at least not here. According to them, we're the ones milking and abusing the system and you know pissing off God so that he comes after everyone. They will keep flying their Rebel flags and supporting the Trump planet-destroying machine not because they are idiots but because they are willfully ignorant. Because of what they "believe" not "know" because that would assume they had studied anything at all. They don't. They watch FOX news and believe only those things that support what they already "believe."

Gratitude is the keystone of happiness? I'm never going to be happy that I—or anyone else—is getting screwed over by a greedy, rich bastard. I'm happy they aren't dragging American citizens from their homes and shooting them in their heads on their front lawns... Yet.

By the time I add my personal problems, heart breaks and failures to the disappointment I have in the country and the human race in general how am I supposed to hang onto any semblance of hope?

How can I expect to rise in the morning and feel anything but the most crushing despair? How? Humans are trying to evolve into something better. I am personally trying to evolve into a better person, but how can I do that here in the Southern US or what I like to call the asshole of hell?

Give up.

What exactly am I supposed to give up or give up on? Doesn't giving up go against the very nature of people who have worked hard and persevered? To admit defeat, to throw up your hands and say, "There is nothing I can do about any of my problems. I must just live on because living on is what is expected of me."

Really? At that point what the hell is the meaning of life? Maybe that's what I need to give up on—the idea that I have a purpose—that anyone does. Maybe we are just like salmon. We come, we spawn, we die, a bear eats us, shits, and fertilizes the earth.

Ahh! The circle of life.

I no longer enjoy any part of my life and I'm too chicken shit to blow my brains out, so now what? Maybe things will get better? Maybe the Universe will care about what is right on some level and fix everything that is broken? In any case I can't do a damn thing about it, so I should just live and let live. *Que sera, sera* and all that good crap.

I don't have control neither does God. Nothing is working for me because I don't have control and neither does God. I can't fix the world. I can't even protect my children. I can't fix my life; I sure as hell can't fix theirs, and trying is making me absolutely crazy. I mean come on—I'm literally talking to myself.

I'm supposed to live with whatever life throws at me without any helpful people in my life. Hell the nicest thing anyone ever did for me was to give me goats that had the plague. How the hell am I supposed to find joy much less gratitude when everything I care about is going to hell in a handbasket?

What are we? Why are we? Why is life pain? Why do assholes get every fucking thing they want? Why do the innocent pay for the sins of the wicked? How do we find hope in a garden of rocks and weeds?

Nothing in my life has worked out to my benefit. My life sucks. Now people on the outside can look in all they like and say it isn't so, but all that matters is my perception that my life sucks. The key to finding the gratitude and through it a sense of contentment is in changing my perspective, but how can I do that when I am losing everything I care about and everything looks hopeless?

I can't. No one can unless they have had something in their life history that was so brilliant that they know that good can happen for them. I don't know that. Any even moderately good thing that has ever happened has been immediately followed by something horrible, so that at this time I fear nothing as much as joy.

That—by the way—sucks ass.

There was a moment during the current debacle which is the ongoing tragedy of my life, in which I just admitted to defeat. I admitted there was nothing I could do, admitted to the defeated, wounded, broken thing inside me that was sure it could never feel happiness or joy again, that I was done.

These days it doesn't take much to send me right into the pit of despair.

I was supposed to pick Avy up to have him for a night and day, but once again Jenny changed her mind at the last minute. It was more than I could handle. I collapsed in the floor and I sobbed and screamed and cried till every bone and muscle in my body hurt. I cried as I had never cried before. My wife—who has never been good at saying or doing anything that helps me—insisted on talking and being in the room with me which just pissed me off so bad I yelled at her as if all my pain was her fault. But seriously, feeling that I had attached myself in a permanent fashion to someone who didn't understand me at all made things worse. I sobbed even harder. I banged my head on the floor. I prayed for death to take me. This went on for an hour till I had leaked all the despair out of me. When I finally got up I felt like I could deal with the new awful. I slept all night for the first time in weeks.

I thought maybe I had finally listened to myself and just given up. That the giving up I was supposed to do was to quit trying to control anything including how I felt and just feel and process the full level of my despair.

Admitting I couldn't fix anything to make my life the way I wanted it, admitting I just had to live with my life the way it was, didn't make me feel any better. It just made me feel resolved. For three days I felt like I had a handle on things. Then I got a phone call that let me know things could get even worse and that what I thought was the new normal wasn't. My adversary had complete control over all I cared about and they could make me even more miserable with the snap of their fingers. See it turned out that letting Jenny know I was unhappy about not having Avy was enough to let her think it was time to tell me off and threaten me with not seeing him at all.

Why I Blame Trump on Jesus

You see I'm not really allowed to feel anything. No matter what is done to me I'm supposed to silently accept it. What did I say that was so horrible? That I missed him and I didn't think it was fair for her to say he could come and then send him somewhere else. You know, I told the truth. I didn't say what I was really feeling which was, "Why don't you die you fucking cunt!" so I really thought I should get a fucking gold medal. Instead I got the queen bitch of us all telling me off over the phone for fifteen minutes while knowing I was already in the weeds. I said nothing at all till she hung up on me—no doubt because I said nothing at all which was offensive to her.

So what did I do? I started to work. I multitasked because if I get enough balls in the air I can't usually focus on my problems. If I'm honest that is what I have always done—just buried myself in usually hard, physical work in an effort to not have any room left in my brain to think about everything that sucks. But it didn't work this time at all. My mind was still on the new, horrible thing that had been done to me, and in the middle of one project but working on another I forgot I had moved a stepping stone to pour a slab (you know because the stepping stone was a tripping hazard—you gottah love irony) I stepped down and twisted my left knee and my right ankle and I broke the lower big bone (no I didn't feel like looking up the technical name—suck it!) in both of my legs. Now I was in the chicken yard and knew no one could hear me. When I could I levered myself up and moved till my back was against the chicken house wall. I looked down and the bottom of my right foot was looking back at me, and my left knee was at a wrong angle. I took a deep breath, reached down and put my foot back where it belonged. Then I waited for that to calm back down, reached down and popped my left knee into place.

That's right: emotionally and mentally I'm a fucking mess, but maybe because of the brutal life I've had when it comes to my ability to take physical pain I'm a fucking bad ass.

Then I sat there dealing with my pain and crying. For the record, I'm usually pretty stoic. The fact that I am crying this much shows how miserable I really am because I wasn't crying because of the pain I was crying because how was I going to get my mind off all my problems if I couldn't work and I was pretty sure both of my legs were broken. I made myself stop crying because that is—after all—for sissies.

My dad used to beat me with a belt. If I would cry he would tell me he'd give me something to cry about, and if I didn't stop crying he would beat me some more, so eventually I learned not to cry. But I am doing it all the time now.

I blame therapy.

"So, dumbass, how's that working out for you?"

I look up at myself. "What?" I ask as I dry away the last of my tears.

"The whole working yourself to death to just not think. How's that working for you?"

"Fuck you. Here's an idea—why don't you do something fucking helpful?"

"Like what?"

"Like remind me I moved the step. Maybe go for help."

"I'm not fucking Lassie. I can't just go in, bark at Liz and have her ask if Timmy fell in the well."

"What the hell can you do?"

"Tell you to give up."

"Alright hot shot that's just what I'm going to do—sit here in the bitter-assed cold in all this chicken shit with my legs broken and pray for death."

"You know that's not what I mean, and it's not what you'll do."

Then the other me just left me there with both my broken-assed legs in the bitter cold.

I think about crying some more but I don't. The truth is just crying never really helps me. I start to deep breath my way through the pain and then I have to deal with the fact that my body is all screwed up and I have no one to blame but myself. There was no part of me that was present when I fell. I wasn't paying attention, and why wasn't I? Because I was worrying about something I couldn't do anything about.

I walked my happy ass up the wall at my back and hobbled back to the milk barn to let the goat in there out. It was only as I was doing this that I realized I should have gone straight to the house because if a goat knocked me over that was just going to make things worse, and I was already in a world of hurt. I hobble in the house and sit in my chair.

Liz comes running in. "Are you alright?"

Seriously, did I look alright? I'd obviously been crying, and I was covered in mud and chicken shit.

I look at her and say very calmly, "No I am not alright. I have sprained my right ankle and my left knee, and I think I have broken both of my legs."

She freaks out because that's what she does; when I need help she falls the fuck apart. But she helps me to the car and takes me to the ER where they proceed to tell me what I already know. They put me in two strap-on walking casts because they can't cast them because the sprains have them swelled up to about four times their size.

I am super pissed off at myself because I had managed to take bad and turn it into even worse and our insurance sucked ass so I didn't know how much this trip to the ER was going to cost. Since we were already as broke as shit I knew damn good and well it was going to be more than we could afford. To make matters worse I hadn't cut nearly enough firewood and that meant we'd have to burn gas which in my opinion was like burning up money.

Mostly though I will be able to do nothing but take care of the livestock which will be a bitch in two walking casts. Why will I have to do it? Because there is no one else to do it. See Liz has never learned to milk. When we first started dating she made it clear that if I wanted to keep living the way I always had that I could take care of the animals and the garden; she wanted no part of it.

Yet I kept dating her. I stayed with her even when it became obvious that she was always going to leave me working without a net, so I have no right to bitch that there isn't a backup plan that there is just me. She told me up front that I was always going to have to do everything; there was no pretense.

Besides which Liz always gets sick any time I am as if physical misery is a competition she must win. In fact, I no sooner sit in the recliner and put my broke ass legs up than Liz announces, "I feel like I'm coming down with something."

Yep, no one to blame but myself.

The next few weeks dragging myself around to do the things that must be done and then sitting and putting my feet up when the pain is too bad becomes an ongoing lesson in how little control I have over my life and how important it is to be present.

When you are all busted up you have to walk with care. You have to slow down; you have to watch where you are going. If I fall again even three weeks later all those cracks that are just starting to heal will become full-blown breaks.

So between the full mental break down and the fall I was starting to sort things out. Then my son's father decided to die again. Now he has had cancer for over ten years and has used it as an excuse to go on cruise after cruise making sure he will leave my son nothing. Every time he has snapped his fingers for that whole time my son has dropped everything in his life to go running to help his father. Let's just say it; my son's father was a *goniff*. He committed many crimes against most everyone he came into contact with. He was a thief, a liar, a cheat, a pervert.

When my father talked him into marrying me to keep me from being queer he was thirty-four; I was sixteen. He married me because I was a virgin and he had never dirtied a virgin. He took me to a drug den in Chicago and bullied me into smoking pot. The pot was laced with God alone knows what, and to this day I can't be a hundred percent sure what he and his friends did to me but I know it wasn't good. I was sixteen years old, and I was already a fucked up mess, but after that I was never the same again.

And he was proud of what he had done.

He was a crappy father to the three kids he was responsible for bringing into this world. His two daughters from his second wife he had moved away from and never had contact with in order to keep from paying child support. He used my son to continue to torture me, but he was never really there for Ryan.

Yet my son dropped everything to run and take care of him as he lay on his deathbed. Levi could have paid for hospice; he did not. He could have gone into a nursing home; he did not. He never changed a diaper on any of his kids, but my son had to change his for three weeks. My son needed to be home with his family, but nothing would do but that bastard turned him into his nurse maid.

I found out this morning that Levi shot himself. I was more surprised that he was really sick than I was that he shot himself. See for the last thirty years of his life he has belonged to the hemlock society—in case you aren't aware of what it is, it's a group that advocates that people should have a right to kill themselves when they are terminal. I don't disagree, but why did Levi support it? Because he never wanted to do what he made my son do. He never wanted to take care of anyone when they were sick, and he never thought *he* would get sick.

Now he had rallied at least six times... You know he said he was dying, got my son and everyone else to jump through hoops for him, and then... miraculously he was alright. But this time he was really dying and he was in pain, so after basically ruining the last three weeks for my son and his family—it was of course the holiday season—he shot himself.

Now why did he shoot himself? He had enough medication on hand to kill a horse and he was a drug addict who loved nothing better than being high. So why shoot himself? Because he never cared about anyone but himself—ever. He was a manipulative control freak. He died without ever admitting to much less apologizing or making amends for—any of the horrible things he did to nearly everyone who had ever cared about him or he had even remote contact with.

At one point in time I not only forgave him—forgiveness is a gift you give yourself—but I actually thought he had changed. That he wasn't the same person. I treated him like a member of the family. He sat at our table, he ate with us, we talked, we laughed. Then Liz and I got married and he showed his whole, entire ass fighting with my friends on Facebook. Everything that was wrong about me and Lynn getting married. Shortly after that my son had his near-fatal motorcycle accident and the bastard said the things he said.

For sixteen hours as I waited in the hospital worried about my only child, this asshole took potshots at me, and my son's wife, and even his own wife. He spent the whole time trying to stir my daughter-in-law and I up so that she would attack me. She she did he could watch with glee—it happened more than once. He told funny stories, laughed, and in short wasn't worried about Ryan at all. Before my son got out of recovery he finally left without talking to him at all. Levi was there for two reasons only: to make me and Jenny as miserable as possible, and to make my son believe that he actually gave a shit at all so that he could continue to use him.

That's who Levi was. I knew in that moment that he hadn't changed at all; he was the same asshole he had always been.

He not only wasn't sorry for any of the things he had done to me, but as he sat there purposely saying things to see if he could trigger me I realized that I had given him human attributes he had never had. He not only didn't care that he had caused everyone in his life pain he delighted in it. He got off on the power he had to make me and everyone else squirm.

How he died proves that. There were pain killers everywhere—he was after all a terminal cancer patient—so why did he shoot himself? He wanted to make one more mess for people to clean up. He wanted people to *know* that he killed himself, thus continuing the abuse he has always heaped on people. The place he killed himself in will be forever ruined for the people he left behind. They will feel varying degrees of guilt. Mostly he had complete control. He always had complete control, and why? Because he was willing to do anything for his own happiness, and he would be the first one to tell you that. The fact that he could die in a way that would make so many people unhappy was classic Levi.

I understand not wanting to die in pain. I do. I don't understand that you are so hateful you actual shoot yourself. He lived a bastard; he died a bastard. And he was happy till he wasn't, and then he killed himself. He never suffered for any of the horrible things he did to me or anyone else. And he killed himself while his wife and my son were in the house, so there is no even pretending that he didn't mean to do as much damage as he possibly could.

He was seventy-seven years old; he wasn't even young. He had always done just exactly what he wanted to do. Except for the cancer nothing bad ever happened to him because he never cared one bit about anyone. Even the cancer he used to get what he wanted till it finally made him actually sick.

So where is the karma in the story of this man's life? I may never get over my PTSD. My financial struggle is entirely his fault because he took everything but my son in the divorce. I built everything Levi kept in the divorce with my own hands while he sat on his ass, smoked grass and did drugs. I did all the work and our entire married life he never allowed me to have more than five dollars at a time. Then he got it all—everything I had ever worked for. He was supposed to pay me seventy-five dollars a month in child support; he didn't even pay that every month. He stole things from me I can never get back—my youth, my peace of mind.

And get this: the mother fucker was rich. Not just because he stole from everyone who was ever stupid enough to have business dealings with him, but because his grandfather had left him a small fortune. He never had to really work—which was good because he was the laziest mother fucker who ever lived.

That's who he was. Yet he lived a charmed life. People liked him—till he used or shafted them. No one ever expected anything of him, no one ever judged him—except me and all the other people he screwed over. In his life the people around him always paid for his sins, and in his death he has found a way to make other people keep paying.

Is there to be no punishment for any of his crimes? Because I don't believe in hell and certainly he didn't pay for his crimes on this planet. Where is he now? Does part of him still exist? In the place where all that is left of him is, does he feel the pain of the people he hurt? Does he wish he had done better? Made amends? Not hurt people? Not used them? Or is his soul such a cesspool that even now he looks at his life and applauds the fact he was always happy no matter who it hurt? That he gained his greatest happiness from giving other people pain and no one ever held his feet to the fire for it?

It doesn't matter. For me and my life it doesn't matter. For those he left behind it doesn't matter. My son hurts because his father is dead. He wants me to hurt because his father is dead and is mad at me because I can't at least pretend to be sad. I did a fucking dance. I just wish I would have let him die a long time ago.

Ryan knows it is better that Levi's dead, but he can't be happy with the way he died. It is something he will now have to carry around. The fact he spent the last three weeks taking care of his father will not remove him from any guilt. Worse than all that unless he can ever admit that his father was the world's biggest asshole he will never forgive himself for his father killing himself.

Levi can only continue to win if I can't let go of my rage.

Someone *please* tell me how to let go of my rage.

Now he's dead there will never be any justice. It's not our place to judge, but when someone ruins us it is hard not to.

He had all the control; this is what he has done, and now my son will not talk to me. That's right. Somehow this is also my fault. No, I didn't say anything hateful about his stinking father, but he must know how I feel and mostly he just doesn't want to talk about it. Who would? So I can't even make an attempt to comfort him and so my son's father has left this world with a big fuck you to everyone.

Both of my legs are broken, my goats have plague, I still look for bugs every fucking night, and my son is mad at me. In fact, he says he needs to talk to me because he is upset by something I have done. So looking forward to that talk. I love being blamed for every fucking thing. The asshole kills himself and he's a big hero. Me? I'm the bad guy again.

I know I am in the very bottom of my pit because I look at what he did and find behind the anger and resentment a layer of envy because I lack the courage to kill myself much less do it in a way that would make those I leave behind have to ask if they should have treated me better.

Chapter Nine

I can't figure out what my purpose is. I thought it was to write fiction, but that was a bottomless pit of need where I found no success. I thought it was to be a mother; I failed at that. In short, everything I have ever done has failed. Now I'm fifty-nine, so good luck doing anything meaningful now. This is the time in your life when you can really only contribute something of worth if you have already succeeded. The time when you are supposed to be able to rest on your laurels—look back and smile at all you have accomplished.

How can I get to a good place when there is no balance?

How do I hang onto anything remotely like contentment in the face of constant failure, when I crawl out of one hole just to fall into another? It is easy for someone to expound on how hardships taught them valuable lessons about life, the Universe, and everything when they got to get out of the hole and live for a few years before they fell in another one. When you have award-winning, bestselling books that made you rich, and people spend hundreds of dollars just to hear you talk... Success makes it easier to dig yourself out of any despair. Knowing what you do matters to others, having enough money to live comfortably, to be able to just run to the doctor when you are sick or buy a new car when the old one is turning to crap, or have the dryer delivered instead of picking it up and not needing the salvage money for the old dryer to help pay for the new one.

The fucking bill for our part of the broken legs is seven hundred dollars. Fuck me!

I have trouble with people who never had to lift a hood when their cars broke down telling me how to fix my car, and I have even more trouble with people who are super successful trying to tell me how I can feed my soul. It's easy to say success and money aren't important when your life overflows with both. Easy to say desire is the root of all pain and I should just not want anything and then I will find contentment when you have everything your heart could ever desire.

As for positive thought bringing all good things into our lives and negative thoughts pulling negativity to us? I'm burned out trying to think good things. Someone who has had a shit life like mine.... You live on hope. Hope that things will get better. You try to see the positive in a world full of negatives, and as I've said, bundle the small nice things into a bundle of good. You give and give and give to others in the hopes it will fill the hole in your life, and what comes back to you? A big nothing. All your bundles of nice—other people kick those apart as fast as they can in an effort to prove that nothing you have ever done has any worth or merit. They remove you from the things you love and let you know in no uncertain terms that you have no control, and somewhere inside you know that control is always just an illusion.

At least it is always ever an illusion for the have-nots. The rich and powerful, the successful, they own you. They control you; *they* have control. It's not easy to be a serf to the corporations, and there is no champion to save us. How can we possibly find any kind of solace any kind of peace at times like these? If your personal life was fine when the ass hat took office, you were upset. If your personal life was a wall-eyed mess, it was the icing on the big shit cake called life.

What can I possibly do right now to lift my spirit and make sense of the cesspool which is my life?

I was out taking care of the goats when she... I... showed up again. In fact, she just followed me as I was carrying water out to pour in the trough.

"Just give up."

"Crap, you again."

"Is it helping to be so mad all the time? Levi's dead. He can't do anything to you now."

"Well you are wrong there because my son is now super mad at me as in he won't talk to me, and I haven't talked on the phone to much less seen Avy in over six weeks. That's all because of Levi."

"No, it's because you won't give up."

Then I was gone. Crap!

I have to give up. Seriously? I've already given up on everything; it's not helping. What's that mean—just give up? Give up; sink into my despair; own my pain? Lay there in the bottom of the pit as long as I have to, cry till I hurt? Cry till I can't anymore, blubber and sob the angry hurt parts of myself out into the void and when I am all cried out take a big breath, sit up look where I am, view the pit all around me and at the top of the pit I see that there is light. It is faint and dull; I've been here before, and I will start climbing.

It gets harder every time because I know there is most probably nothing I really want at the top, but at least it isn't so dark. The climb is the journey out of the darkness into the light, but there are no promises in the light. It will not bring me instant healing or gratification. Many times even as I'm climbing out of the top of the hole an army of assholes is waiting to let me know it was a wasted effort that I should have stayed where I was.

Really what's the point?

Right now it just seems easier to lie in the bottom of the pit and look up at the light. There is more promise in the unknown. If I fight my way to the top only to be crushed again... Well, this might be the time I just can't take it.

But you do keep working, Oliva said.

"Last time I looked things didn't get done because good fairies come and do them because I'm having a bad day, year, life."

"Somewhere in you, you must know that doing nothing isn't the answer or you wouldn't even be here."

How is that helpful? I wonder, but just say the truth. "I literally have no one else to talk to... no one who gives a shit what happens to me. Why should I climb up and then walk through all the assholes when chances are I will just fail again? I'm less of a target for anyone in the bottom of the pit. What's the point of crawling out just to get kicked back in again? You know what my crappy life has taught me? Assholes get whatever they want out of life and the innocent pay for their crimes—always. There is no justice. I can try to push those thoughts out of my head, but you know what? That doesn't feel healthy; it feels like lying to myself. Negative thoughts are bad and positive thoughts are good; that's what they all say. But are they right? I don't think so. If I walk around being super up and positive and thinking that only good things will happen for and to me and then a super crappy thing happens, I'm not ready for it not at all. And if anytime I have even an ounce of joy something horrible happens—then I fear joy."

"Maybe you need to learn how to accept joy when it happens." She's a good therapist because she isn't detached; she actually cares. And I know what she means, but I'm not ready to hear it.

"I don't get to keep any light I find because it is always smothered by the darkness. Some asshole always snatches it away and then the darkness is that much darker. How do you suggest I keep from falling into life's gaping crevasses? Stop caring about anybody or anything? Don't have a relationship, and whatever you do don't have kids. Get rich; be super successful; don't worry about the people you will have to hurt or kill to get there. Don't worry about anyone but yourself, and you can accomplish whatever you want. In short, be a selfish douche, and if I am I will be truly happy. Being the perpetual nice guy certainly isn't working for me. Maybe I should just tell everyone to take a flying fuck!"

"You should learn to tell people no because you shouldn't let people use you. You deserve better than that."

"But I can't because I have always had to live under the rule that if I can't make them love me I will make them need me."

Olivia says seemingly out of the blue, "I want you to try EMDR therapy for your PTSD. It uses light pulses to trick the brain into REM sleep which allows the brain to process trauma and then let it go. I am currently taking the classes and should be certified in a few months, so think about it." She hands me a brochure, and my session is over.

Don't desire anything; desire causes pain. But if it doesn't hurt you who cares, right?

I have lived my life working hard to do no harm. The result is I am now a huge gaping wound and no one—not one single person—actually gives a shit about me or how I feel. Every thought I have, every step I take is pain. Losing the enlightenment I had spent a lifetime to attain... Well that is a pain I haven't found a way to deal with. I just keep trying and getting so close and then... I just keep falling into more holes. Why? Because I have attached myself to people who don't give a shit about me or how I feel.

I have always been a fighter. I have never been happy to just lie in the bottom of the pit. I have always worked to crawl out, but now... I'm running out of fight and so tired of looking at the half-empty glass and proclaiming it is half full. Oh it's half full alright! Half full of shit!

There are children in concentration camps on our border. They have been ripped away from their parents and imprisoned. Some of them have died. Forever those children will have to deal with what that ass hat in the

White House has done. And he doesn't care; he doesn't care about thousands of children living with the same but different PTSD nightmare that has shaped my life. What can I do about it? Nothing!

Without money, without a platform,, without respect, how can I make a difference at all? What is my purpose can I even have a purpose when I don't have any control of anything? Without purpose what is the meaning of anything?

Maybe if I shot myself in the head my son would finally think I'm a big hero.

If I have NO control and can't really stop any of the injustices I see, if in fact I am the recipient of those injustices, what is the point of me? Pain? Is it just about my pain? Does my pain somehow amuse the Universe; does it give the Universe something it needs wants or desires?

Levi killed himself because he couldn't live with pain. Will I kill myself when I can't deal with the pain? Is that the message future me is trying to give me—that I must fix myself before I kill myself?

If my soul is here to learn things, what does it learn from a lifetime of regrets and pain? Bitterness? How will that help the Great Communal Soul? How does that help anyone or anything?

Is it ever enough to just exist? To exist when hope is gone is hard. Hope leaves when life has been a series of holes you must climb out of to keep going toward a destination you can't see. I can no longer make a simple decision, why? Because everything I have ever done has failed. I no longer trust myself to choose a destination and move towards it because everything I have ever done has brought me to this moment in time, and at this moment in time I could be more miserable, but I would have to actually work at it.

When my son's father could stand his pain no longer he shot himself and everyone will understand that because he was dying anyway. But depression is the ultimate pain. It is the death of the spirit, but no one ever gives the depressed person a pass when they kill themselves. Yet that level of depression is often caused by the very people who in life made them so miserable and who in death are the first ones to damn them.

The cure for depression is not a pill or even therapy. The cure for depression is to have something actually good happen for you. When nothing really good ever does—or worse yet when it does and someone ruins it for you—you don't trust anything good. You don't trust love, or joy, or even happiness because if your truth is that the minute you do someone rips it from you... then nothing scares you as much as love or joy or even happiness. You wind up scared shitless of the things you most want.

People who can live in the moment, you know that their past is not a minefield of bad choices, regrets and trauma. They can live in the moment because the moment has never truly slain them. Their spirit is still alive; they still feel worthy; they still love themselves.

Or they had something traumatic happen but they lived and then things got really good, better than they were before the trauma. So they easily live in the present letting go of the past not worried about the future.

They say the key is to love yourself. It is not true that you can't love others if you don't love yourself. That's a bullshit thing people say to try to make you feel even more broken. They say it to make you feel even more worthless because maybe then you will fix yourself.

Someone making me you feel worse about yourself never helped me on any level. It doesn't help me for the stupid-assed people in my life to tell me that I have nothing to be depressed about. It doesn't help for them to point out all the mundane pluses I have going for me or to tell me that my depression is selfish.

I have friends who get depressed and they fucking do nothing. They sit on their asses, whine, and expect everyone in their life to take care of them. I don't do that. I just work myself into a stupor. I not only do everything

I'm supposed to do, I do a million things I don't have to do and many—sometimes most—of those things are for other people. To help other people.

If you love yourself enough other people can't really hurt you. But good luck loving yourself if no one has ever really loved you the way you need to be loved. Good luck loving yourself if you are always at the bottom of everyone's love list.

What's a love list? Here's a big lie people tell, they will say they love people the same. That's a bullshit. Even when parents say they love their children the same this is a lie. It is commendable when they manage to hide that they have a favorite, but make no doubt that they always do. Why? Because we are always going to love people more who love us more. When everyone in your life loves you less than they love others... good luck building up any self-love. I can't love myself if no one has ever loved me enough for me to know how it feels to have real love. Good luck loving yourself when everyone in your life has gone out of their way to make sure you know there is something wrong with you that makes you—if not completely unlovable—less loveable.

They tell you everything about you is wrong and then the fact that they love you at all makes them good people because, after all, you are really unlovable.

I have done all the 'loving yourself' exercises. Looking in the mirror for thirty days telling my reflection I loved me—I didn't manage to do that one even one time that I didn't feel like a complete idiot, so that wasn't helpful. Hugging myself telling me I love me—still doing that one, not working at all, and again I feel like a huge idiot while I'm doing it.

I get things mostly figured out, I move close to getting back the contentment I lost, and then well something else crappy happens and never, never does the really good thing happen to cause balance.

I live with someone so completely self-centered that she can say or do nothing to help me because part of what she needs from me is to have someone she can come home to that she can always feel superior to. That isn't as good as her, see that helps her with her self-worth—you know that she is married to someone who is beneath her station.

In not so many words my therapist has told me that this is my own shitty perception, but here's the problem: can my wife not do something that changes my perspective so that I believe she actually cares about me enough to want to help me out of my pain without making my depression all about her?

Now she would tell you that isn't true at all, and most people who know us would tell you that isn't true at all, but that's the way her actions make me feel. Now there is a whole school of thought that says I am in control of the way I feel and that I shouldn't blame anyone else for the crappy way they make me feel because it is my fault not theirs that I feel that way.

That seems like a whole lot of double talk to me.

Here's what I hear when people talk that shit. Because I'm big and fat, gay and ugly, broke and a failure, and therefor wrong in every way, I must carefully watch the things I do or say to others. But they can treat me any way they want to. I'm not supposed to want to be treated with respect or love. I'm supposed to be always happy with the scraps thrown my way and sleeping outside alone in the cold, but the glass is half full and I need to love myself enough.

Tell me how? Don't tell me to do something; tell me *how* to do it.

The world is a dark, hard place when you aren't successful or good looking. The human race acts as if the fact they allow me in their space should be enough. That I shouldn't expect that people will love me with their whole heart, respect me, or go out of their way in any way, shape, or form for me because *I'm* the thing that is wrong. The awful way people treat me, the disregard they have for me, is my fault because I'm not pretty, or normal, or successful.

And I'm not so different, am I? Lots of people live with the guilt and the shame that comes from being born "wrong." They are also the black sheep in their family, the thing that made their parent scream at and or beat them. It was always all my fault when my dad got angry. I made him hit me, and if I cried he was right to give me something to cry about. If I stopped crying and he kept hitting me? Well that was my fault, too. If only I weren't so stupid or weak, if only I was less clumsy, prettier, more like a real girl.

It's not my fault that I can't just build a whole butt load of self-love and a sense of worth, any sense of contentment. Where would I have learned, *ever* learned, that it was alright to be me, that I deserved love? I spent my whole life trying to be perfect so that maybe people wouldn't treat me like crap. So that maybe they would love me more. I spent my whole life trying to do something huge because maybe then people wouldn't see the shameful *wrongness* of me. I needed to accomplish something so huge that no one could ever look down on me again. But all I did was fail, and with every failure people judged me harder and maybe... If I had never tried to do anything but just exist at least I wouldn't be so tired now.

All of that wasn't helping. All that the running dialogue in my head was doing was making me worse. I was magnifying all the horrible, but really I couldn't downplay it anymore. I was tired of pretending that things were going to magically get better—or worse yet— were already alright.

It wasn't alright; none of it was.

I was milking and all that crap was going through my head because I was dealing with the sick goats with my broke-assed legs in the bitter cold and my son said he needed to "talk" to me because I had done something terrible. I had no idea what that was, and until he was ready to confront me he didn't want to talk to me at all.

Yes, but I'm a controlling bitch.

"Wow! I didn't remember that I was ever this low."

I couldn't face me this time. I didn't even look up from where I was milking.

"Shut up and go away," I hissed.

"Why? I couldn't possibly make you feel any worse."

"Yes you can because you're going to tell me to give up but not tell me exactly what you mean and I'm wracking my brain trying to figure it out."

"Because you want to get better."

"I at least want to get well enough that I'm not hallucinating your ugly ass."

"You talk to yourself a whole lot worse than you'd let anyone—but maybe your son and his wife—talk to you."

"They hold all the cards."

"Eventually you're going to have to reshuffle the deck and get new cards."

"Great! Now you sound like that fucking enlightenment of the day calendar my wife bought me for Chanukah."

"Where do you think I learned it? She's trying to help."

"And failing abysmally."

"It's your fault because you won't give up."

Then I was gone again.

We lie to the world in the hope they won't see the damaged, unworthy person we are trying so desperately to hide. We judge ourselves far more harshly than the rest of the world does and why is that? Because we were taught to hate ourselves. The parents, the families, the schools who we are told are supposed to nurture us and get us ready for adulthood... I never got that. Other people did but not me. Even that makes me feel like I am the crap under other people's feet. Because what is so wrong with me that I wasn't born into a family where I would be loved and cherished? Why could I not get the teachers who uplifted me instead of the ones who stuck me at the slow table and told me—maybe in not so many words—"You are stupid."

I have been treated like trash my whole life. Not always, and not by everyone, but I have never had a moment in my life when I wasn't forced to be attached to someone who seemed to live for every moment that they could make me feel inferior and miserable.

It's not my fault that I can't get out of the pit and stay out of the pit. It's the fault of everyone who lashes out and never apologizes. It's the fault of all the people who have always judged me and told me I was a piece of worthless shit. I know, alright? I've read it in many books; I shouldn't take someone else's dysfunction personally. Good luck with that when they are yelling in your face and opening all the wounds from your youth.

It isn't my fault that other people are assholes. You know what? I didn't fail them... they failed me. They always wanted more from me than I could ever realistically do, and all I wanted was for them to love me. They couldn't even get that right, so I didn't fail them; they failed me.

They failed *me*.

Not on purpose.

They failed me because of the broken parts of them they could never fix.

"What happened to you?" Olivia asks me as I hobble in and take a seat on the couch. I put my cane down as quickly as I can because I know I'm crazy and a crazy person with anything they might use as a weapon is intimidating to anyone—maybe especially a shrink.

"I fell. I didn't re-break my legs, but I did screw that ankle up again."

"Is that why you haven't been in?"

I had canceled my last three appointments.

"You know what I hate? All the fucking handicapped parking spots; I think one or two is enough. I also think they should just be for people in wheelchairs. Ever since I screwed up both my legs, everywhere I go there are parking spaces right up front that I can't use because I don't have a thingy hanging in my window. Meanwhile, half of them are empty and every fucking time as I am hobbling in from my spot on the back forty some asshole is getting out of their car in the handicapped spot and they aren't having nearly as much trouble getting around as I am. I'm all for making it easier for handicapped people, but why so many spots? And when did it cover every ailment known to man, and if it does I shouldn't have to have a sticker? When both my fucking legs are broken I ought to be able to use one of those spots."

Olivia smiled. "Why haven't you been in?"

"I just don't know that anything is going to help me, and even the copay seems like an awful lot of money if it isn't going to make me better. It's not you; it's me," I add with a half grin.

"So why are you here then?" she asks carefully, no doubt because of the cane/weapon.

I take a big breath and let it out then answer truthfully. "Liz made me come. She said I have to have help." And so I caught her up with everything that had happened and when I did I think she clearly saw why I thought nothing would help.

"Why do you think Ryan blames you for what his dad did?"

"Because he as much as said so. He hates me. He blames me for everything from his drug abuse to his father blowing his brains out and everything in between. I failed my own son because of the broken parts of me I couldn't fix. I lashed out at times—not because he had done nothing—he had in every case, but I overreacted because I was a head case. He doesn't forgive me, and so as an adult he now abuses me in the same way my father did. He lashes out often tearing my personality and everything I believe in apart. He withholds his love when he is unhappy with me or with his own life, because he holds me directly responsible for everything that is wrong in his life because my choices affected him in negative ways. Maybe he's right. Maybe it is all my fault.

"He gives the father thing a complete pass and never holds him accountable for anything and yet me? I have apologized and tried to make amends. He treats me like crap—worse than that he lets his wife lose her shit on me whenever she feels like it. Then he took his son and moved so that he made a huge child-sized hole in my heart. But I'm just supposed to accept that every stupid, fucking thing he says and does is golden.

"People always tell me how wonderful, helpful and kind a man he is and yet... He has been so cruel to me that it is hard for me to even breathe at least part of every day.

"Ryan is just trying to live his life. I'm an easy target for his aggression because he knows I will love him and be right there if he needs me no matter what he does or says to me. And his wife? Well she has Avy to use as an emotional hostage, so she can just rip me a new one and tear me completely down any time she feels like it because I have to kiss her ass."

"How is any of that your fault?"

"It's not, but well I think how bad it makes me feel is. If I were a 'normal' human I wouldn't like the things they do to me, but it wouldn't just ruin my whole life, would it? A normal human would scream back and then let it go or not scream back and let it go. It wouldn't loop and loop and loop. They wouldn't blame themselves over and over and over again.

"I did the best I could in my brokenness. I gave Ryan everything I had to give, and I never had anything for myself. I love him through all he has done to himself and to me. He loves me only when it is convenient for him to do so, and then just a little. He and his wife have continued the pattern of abuse I have had to deal with my whole life. On a regular basis they point out everything that is wrong with me. My son has told me over and over the same story about the three times I just lost my shit with him. I have apologized a hundred times. I am sorry.

"Everyone who ever hurt me... none of them ever paid. All of them were forgiven not just by me but by everyone else. The crappy things they did—all forgiven. Even the crimes they committed—all forgiven. But any of the mistakes I made, my bad choices, my moments of rage—all of those get used any time my son is unhappy. When a dog craps on the rug the old 'go to' was to rub his nose in it. When someone attacked someone over something stupid they did my dad always said they rubbed his nose in it. My dad used me as a whipping boy; he married me off when I was sixteen to a thirty-four-year-old drug addled pervert to keep me from being gay. I didn't want to rub his nose in it; I just wanted him to admit the way he treated me was wrong and apologize for what he did. That would release me from thinking that *I* was what was wrong. He couldn't do that; he never did that. To do so would be admitting that he was wrong, that the way he treated me was wrong, and if the way he treated me was wrong then I'm not worthless.

"So I apologized to my son. I told him I was wrong. I did it right after I did it, I have done it a hundred times since and what happened? Because I admitted what I did was wrong he beats me with it. I gave him the thing I always needed and in doing so gave him the tools to continue to abuse me in the way my father and then my husband did. To just whale on me with a rod built of the wrongness of me.

"Maybe that is why my father never apologized. Maybe he knew what he did was wrong. He once started a fight with me because someone else said something about the way he treated me. He assumed I had told this person something. I had not. He proceeded to go on a thirty-minute tirade about how I was a SCAN reject. How I was a grown woman and no one cared about the things I said he did. He never tied barbed wire around my head or beat me with a board with nails in it, so I just needed to get over it."

"You can't just get over it. You have to work through it," Olivia said.

"I'm trying, I really am, but I just can't handle even one more thing. No one who has ever caused me pain has ever owned any part of it. They always blamed everything they did to me on me. I have toxic guilt because I made a handful of bad memories for my son, but no one cares when they hurt me."

"Most survivors of child abuse don't talk about it. It's traumatic. You didn't tell when you were little because you were afraid and you didn't believe anyone could make it stop because when you are a kid your parents are in control. Then there is that other thing—you love your parents no matter what they do to you. You still love them because a child's love for their parents is unconditional. And the truth is kids naturally feel like whatever is happening in their house is happening everywhere." That was more than Olivia usually said in three sessions. Maybe she was catching up for all the weeks I missed.

"The biggest problem was that my father wasn't a bastard all the time. He could be the neatest, kindest, most nurturing person in the world. Then I would make the wrong noise or get the wrong look on my face, he'd be mad at someone else, or I'd fail him in one way shape or form, and he would beat the living crap out of me and tell me what a worthless, stupid piece of crap I was— sometimes for hours. Actually the beatings weren't as bad as all the words."

I was in my forties before I ever told anyone but those I was closest to what I'd been through. Why don't grown people talk about the abuse they endured as children? Because the part of them that such abuse breaks is still broken. If there wasn't something wrong with me why would I be treated like that? If it wasn't wrong why wouldn't he apologize and try to do better? I know that everyone sometimes does things they aren't proud of because I have. At least three times I completely lost it with my son. I only spanked him three swats with my open hand each time, but I yelled at him, and like I said the words hurt worse. He remembers none of the good things I did, but still remembers in detail every shitty thing I ever did or said. He still gets mad and tells me I was a shitty mother because of it.

Yet he has both spanked and yelled at Avy. He doesn't think he traumatized him, and honestly neither do I. I have never so much as yelled at Avy. I know better now, so I do better.

Why am I always the whipping boy? Am I just being over-sensitive or dramatic? I am very different and without any successes to point to, without accolades that can be easily seen, smelled, tasted, felt or heard my differentness makes me a target. The big, gangly, awkward kid who is so obviously gay—my father would tell me when I finally came out at nearly forty that he had known since I was three—is easy for a parent to take out their frustrations on. I'm fifty-nine. When I was a kid people would have sooner told you their child was a murderer than that they were gay. When my father arranged a marriage for me I went along with it. Why? Because there was no part of me that wanted to be gay, in fact, I pretended to be a huge homophobe so that no one would know—because I still had no desire to dress or act like a girl.

It was a horrible thing for him to do; he should have known what my husband would do to me, how he would treat me. But let's face it I was so used to being abused I was a perfect wife for a man like that. I would have already been screwed up if my dad hadn't arranged that horrible farce of a marriage, but being married to someone who abused me in new and terrible ways just finished me off. My father didn't mean to destroy me— ever. He wanted me to be someone he could be proud of, but he never could be because I was so *wrong*. He loved me, so he needed me to be someone besides me so that he could be proud of me, too.

That will screw you up in ways you can't imagine—the knowledge that people have done awful things to you because they love you but don't like what you are. That will do almost as much damage as living with a woman-hating, controlling bastard who loves nothing more than to make other people unhappy. Stack one on top of the other and trying to find anything approaching a normal psyche can be impossible.

With my fucked-up background, the fact that I don't just lay around and rot ought to be commendable. It isn't. Why? Because no one believes me. When I tell someone what I have lived through, their go to isn't compassion, it is to disbelieve me. They don't say that, but you can see it in their eyes. Why? Because they couldn't live through what I did and be anything but a douche bag, so they don't believe that I could because of course ten minutes after they first met me they had already judged me and found me wanting because what I am isn't socially acceptable. They couldn't have lived through it without being dysfunctional, so someone like me sure as hell couldn't, therefore I must be making shit up.

I live in Jesusland, the Buckle of the Bible Belt, the American South. Sixty percent of the people here voted for Trump. Forty-seven percent are still happy that they did and they think he is not just a good president but the best one ever. *Booyah!* These people are everything some folks get mad at people for saying Trump voters are. They are racist, they are homophobes, they believe in a woman's right to make her husband dinner and take care of babies—and yes, that includes the women. When there is a mass shooting they don't give a fuck about how many lives were lost or all the families that will be destroyed because of the violence done against them. Nope, all they ever care about is that some liberal is going to try to take their guns away. They continue to do this as the bodies stack higher and higher even though not a single gun law has come even close to passing. In Australia they banned assault rifles and now... they don't have mass shootings. Yet banning them here "won't keep the criminals from getting them and I need guns to hunt." These people never let facts get in the way of them being irate over their second amendment rights. As people's blood covers the ground and the bodies aren't even cold all they can talk about is protecting their rights.

They are alright with children in concentration camps because, "The damned illegals are using up our tax money and taking our jobs." Of course most of the ones bitching the loudest neither work nor do they want to work; they are on welfare, but...

...*I'm* what's wrong and *you're* what's wrong, and everyone who doesn't pray to Jesus, or who believes in a woman's right to choose, or that (God forbid!) we don't need automatic weapons and thirty-round banana clips... is wrong. You know, wrong with a capital "R."

If I had a dime for every time someone here introduced me and said I was either crazy, queer and or Jewish—but I was "alright"—I'd have enough money I wouldn't care what they think. They serve me up as if I need a disclaimer.

Whenever people see you as "the other," you're the first one to catch shit when they are having a bad day, the first one to be suspect if something goes wrong, and the first one they toss aside when they make newer more acceptable friends. In the family you will be ALWAYS the one who is expected to put aside your principles "for the good of everyone else." You will have to apologize if you dare to screw up, but they will not be expected to do anything but show up—especially if the person they have slighted is you.

Trump is president because he was able to get the people who already judge everyone but themselves to turn against everyone that is different from them. He was able to tap into that lowest of human traits: the ability to see danger in the face of someone who is different than we are.

What is wrong with the world is what is wrong with this country and is what makes so many of us unhappy with our lives. We see bad things happening and bad people doing them and we have no control over what is done to us, so how can we hope to do anything to save our country or the world?

We feel powerless, and that is never a good feeling. Because you see most of us are basically good, and good people hate injustice. We aren't alright with people being shot everywhere, or kids in cages, or white supremacists spewing hate and driving into crowds. We don't believe that there are "good people on both sides."

Chapter Ten

"And this is what is most bothering you today?" Olivia asks.

"Yes, you would think with my own life being such a mess that I couldn't possibly be worried about the nation much less the world. But the truth is the worse my life gets the more I see everything as a personal affront. I think a lot of people—not just me—have given up because even if my personal relationships were fantastic, my health was good, and I could pay all my bills what's the point because the cracker in the White House and all his friends in the house and senate have already passed laws that are going to fuck us all over for generations to come unless someone could stop them and we had a good man in office who accomplished—not a damn thing. So I don't have real answers. I just know nothing good can come from the Trump presidency. Let's face it; as a president he is a really crappy celebrity TV star. What did the millions of idiots that voted for him really think he was going to do, and why don't they get that he is fucking them the hardest and the fastest as they continue to near worship him?

"The people that voted for him did so because they believe that he will get rid of all of us that are such a problem because we're different. Hell put us—and all woman kind—back in our proper place and then there will be plenty to go around for all the white Christian men and their obedient women folk. They are way too stupid to understand that they will become the slaves that will grease the machine of the rich. We are to be the grease."

"So who are you really mad at?"

It was a good question. Who really is to blame?

"The Religious Right has always been very easy to lead. All it takes is someone bombastic enough to promise they will give them everything by getting rid of everyone who God hates. They don't tout it much, but the truth is they believe that God hates—but he doesn't hate them—so it has to be all these 'sinners.' And by the way they get to decide what makes someone a sinner and then persecute them. They are mostly hateful to the very core of their being, so why wouldn't they take such a deal? People who are different, we've often seen the worst someone like Trump has to offer, and while they may have kicked us till we just don't feel like getting up anymore we will rise; we always do. It isn't the cookie-cutter people who stand up and get counted, not those who follow a party line or act like one ball team is more worthy than another. The people who don't fit, the ones kept on the outside and picked last, we are used to getting our asses kicked. We have been in the bottom of the pit so many times we know every speck of dirt, every pebble, every hand hold by name. We aren't so easy to control because you see we aren't used to winning. What life has made us really good at is making the best of a bad thing. We're tired of doing it, but we not only know how, we do it really well."

"So… this week you are basically mad at everyone and everything?" Olivia says with a smile.

"Yes exactly and I have no idea what if anything I should do but I'm tired of doing nothing."

"So what happened? You know besides the mass shooting and all that—what happened to you this week?"

I took a deep breath and let it out. "I had to shoot that young doe. I thought she had stopped stumbling, and I thought maybe she was going to be asymptomatic like her mother, but she started spinning on Monday and by Tuesday she couldn't walk. So I had to put her down. I had gone ahead and bred my two older does before this doe's mother tested positive. So if they drop does—which the last two cycles I managed to get two does both of which wound up with CAE—so if they have does and if I catch them when they are falling out I can wait for six months, test them, and see if I still have a herd. But after I had to shoot Hope..."

"Wait! The goat's name was Hope?" Olivia never interrupts me like that.

"Yes, I named her that because I hoped it was the end of the plague and the beginning of better times. See? I told you the Universe is fucking with me. Anyway after I finished burying her I saw my other does and I wished I hadn't bred them that I had just given them to someone who needed brush goats and given on having goats at all. Now I have to wait and see."

"I'm very sorry. That is a lot to deal with."

"You know what I hate?"

Olivia smiled. "Everything?"

I laughed and nodded. "Yes mostly, but in particular I hate it when people win a competition or get an award and they say to the masses at large, 'Never give up on your dreams; if you want it bad enough you can get anything you want.' I want those people boiled in their own pudding with a sprig of holly through their heart. In other words, Bah Humbug. It's a fucking humbug. For every moron who gets their heart's desire, there will be thousands of people just as deserving—maybe more so— who will get nothing but the slime trail those people leave in their wake. Not only can I not make it as a writer, but I can't even make it as a goat farmer. I have given up on all my big dreams, and now it's clear I can't even have the little ones."

"Did you read up on EMDR therapy?"

She knows me; of course I did. I didn't just read the pamphlet she gave me, I got on the web, I talked to friends of mine who worked as therapists—the whole shebang. I take a deep breath and let it out.

"Yes. And yes I want to do it. I've been looking at the list, and I admit I am doing everything on it right now."

She had given me a list when I first started going to her that explained unhelpful ways of thinking. I had it on my fridge. I looked at it all the time, and I was still doing at least one, and sometimes many of them at the same time. In fact "all or nothing," "disqualifying the positive," and "magnification" were on speed dial in my brain, followed by "personalization," "mental filtering" and "over generalizing." And I did all the others, too, just not as often.

"As soon as I get my certification papers and the equipment let's do it. That should give you plenty of time to think about it and work up to it."

Like I said, she knows me.

It's hard enough to handle difficult times, the loss of a loved one, losing a job, physical trauma, sickness, family drama, heartbreak, all of the above, and hold onto a sense of contentment and connection between you and the oneness of the Universal Energy. When you add living in a country we loved which is now a festering hole where people shoot each other in the dozens and other people answer by buying more of the guns those people were just killed with, where people want to frack and drive huge gas-guzzling cars as climate change rips us apart and our leaders insist on saying "not our fault," life becomes unbearable for a thinking, feeling, caring person.

Our answer can't be to just tune out and do nothing, can it? Sitting and doing nothing as the world crumbles around me isn't bringing me any form of balance or peace. But is there anything—anything at all—that I can do about anything?

In the face of a tyrant in the White House who periodically gets his Twitter stick and pokes an even crazier tyrant and threatens nuclear obliteration as my family and my life falls apart, how the hell can I walk my way out of despair?

Desire causes pain; I accept that.

How can you expect me not to desire peace, contentment, health, family harmony? It just doesn't seem like that much to ask. I give up on fame and fortune, but how about a little peace of mind, just a little.

What do I do, what do I do? Don't tell me to meditate and calm down and things will get better. I've done all that. My heart still hurts; I have no hope. Trump just keeps doing crazy-assed, hateful shit and my neighbors all crow as if it is going to somehow trickle down to them. My personal life is a huge mess and I have no friends good enough that I can talk to them, so I have a shrink I can't really afford which is mostly paid for by the insurance I have to have—that I can't really afford.

I made my life about taking care of my grandson—and I admit I did that no one made me do it; I wanted to—and they took him and moved. They aren't that far way, but now I haven't seen him at all in nearly two months because my son is mad at me because his father killed himself. And because... you know... I refuse to pretend to be sad about it. Now I'm a pretty good actress, but that is way beyond my acting chops.

If my son ever gets over his mad we will see Avy like normal grandparents get to see their grandkids. That would be fine if I hadn't been mostly part-time raising him since he was born. My heart is broken and I have no idea what to do with my life because this, this thing that I am doing right now, writing... well I know this is a huge waste of time, heart, and energy... but since they took my kid away and my goats are all dying of CAE and I can hardly walk right now what the hell else can I do? I can sit around and watch fucking TV. I've been doing that for most of a month; I'm sick of it!

Hell they have made me so crazy that periodically a future version of my dead self is haunting me—which honestly that can't be really happening but right now it seems like the most real thing in my life.

I have to do something. I have to find a purpose because otherwise everyone will see how worthless I am, and then what?

Then what?

Nothing at all will change. Whether I sit and do nothing or get up and work till I drop my own history has proven that nothing will get better. If I'm lucky, if I bust my ass I will be able to obtain and hold onto mediocrity. Anything that brings me joy... the things that bring me joy are never controlled by me, so they are there and then someone or something will rip them away.

Remember when I talked about love lists? Well I realized that's why not having Avy always with me is killing me. I was always on the top of Avy's love list. He made me feel worthy in a way I hadn't since his father was a child and I was on the top of *his* love list. You know before Levi programed him to think I was a worthless moron.

I'm losing my ever-loving mind because I finally had someone who loved me the way I wanted to be loved and it gave me a sense of worth and now... well now I don't have that.

I don't matter. I never did. If I don't matter what is the point of me and if there is no point of me why am I here? When you take care of a child you are needed. The child needs you and feeling needed gives me a sense of worth.

I am struggling to find the answer to something I have never found an answer to. How do you dig yourself out of the hole when you have nothing to hold on to? The answers others have given seem like bad bumper stickers. It makes me feel like they have never cared enough about anyone to experience real pain. The whole "give it to God" thing that people are always saying helped them. They never tell *why* it helps them. You know why not? Because the answer is apparently just give up, and I've already explained I don't know what that means and I'm no closer to figuring it out. When people "give a problem to God" they are admitting that they have no control. They know God doesn't either but trust that the Universe will somehow make things turn out right. It usually does not. Most people who pray never get what they pray for. They make it anyway, but maybe they are never as whole, complete, or happy as they put on. Maybe they are afraid to say God let me down. Maybe they are afraid to admit that in fact they let themselves down—or someone else did.

Maybe every poor motherfucker on the planet is just as big a head case as me. After all most people have no idea I'm this screwed up. Most people would never believe I have any level of depression, or that I talk to my future dead self. People who like me think I have it together, and people who don't like me didn't like me the moment they met me because I was queer, Jewish, or both.

Bad things happen. It's not personal, but you still have to deal with it. People do crappy things; they are rewarded. We also have to live with this truth, but we don't have to like it, and we don't have to say "he deserved to win at our expense." We're allowed to say how we feel and allowed to feel what we feel.

Garth Brooks gets to thank God for unanswered prayers because he has a good life. Those of us who have suck lives wish God had answered our prayers and given us just what we wanted.

It's just not how God works. Like I said, God loves without caring. My son loves me but doesn't care what happens to me. Let me tell you something about that kind of love: you don't feel it; it doesn't warm you. People give God human attributes because they need a touchy-feely someone to give them a spiritual hug. Good luck with that shit!

God's compassion is not like our compassion. God slings us out onto a planet and says "Look! I gave you everything you need." Like a parent that gives their child all they could ask for but withholds the comfort that comes from a hug... that is God.

Where is the warm, cuddly god that people talk about? They made that god up. He's a person, and he loves us and only wants the best for us. He made us—and of course in their version of god some people have to be more worthy than others or how do you explain that bad things happen to people who don't appear to deserve it and assholes get whatever they want? We don't like that; it goes against our sense of justice. So now that they have built a nice, relatable god, they have to build heaven and hell so that bad people who were so happy here will be punished for what they did by an evil god—also of their making—and good people who had shit lives will get to be rewarded.

What's so wrong with that—the friendly, just-like-us, relatable, touchy-feely god with the torture chamber for bad people and paradise for those deserving? And none of that happens till you're good and dead. Suffer here, good stuff to follow.

What sort of god tempts people to "test them" then tortures people for the sins they committed on earth for all eternity? And when you look at the long list of things religious nut jobs think are sins.... Seems like everyone is going right straight to hell, do not pass Go, do NOT collect your two-hundred dollars.

We can't have that. Our god has gone from being all touchy-feely to being really sadistic really quickly. Now we have to have an out, so their touchy-feely god dies for them and now they can sin all they want. As long as they say this guy is their god, everything is alright.

According to this belief Jeffery Dahmer is going to heaven, but a Buddhist Monk who spent his life in meditation and doing acts of love and kindness... well he's burning in hell.

Now many people are quite alright with this. I am not one of them. It seems like an awful lot of work to go to because we don't like a God who doesn't intercede on our behalf and who can't be described or contained.

But here's the bold, unfiltered, no-one-wants-to-think-about-it truth. Touchy-feely, nearly-like-us god who cares so much about every little bird and flower and who is supposed to shelter us from harm and evil.... That god doesn't actually exist. So when bad things happen it sends us right to a place of shame because if God didn't sweep in to protect us it must be because we are bad people, deserving of being punished.

This doesn't actually work. It's a bullshit.

When I was a kid my father didn't care whether we believed anything or not. Mother had been raised in our local Temple which was actually two towns away and a thirty-minute car ride one way. Her family only went occasionally, and they never even pretended to be Kosher except during Passover when we weren't even allowed to have a peanut or drink a soda. My siblings and I went to temple maybe three times a year. Mother lit candles some Friday nights but not all. We celebrated Chanukah at home and Christmas with my father's family.

My father's family were happily lapsed Catholics. While they still considered themselves Christian, none of them ever went to church. Let's face it; we all know what happened to Dad. No one ever talked about it, but my dad was agnostic and his whole family had left the church, so we know. It's why I was able to forgive my dad. Someone broke him, and having a kid who was an obvious queer triggered his crap... now didn't it? It was bad, but he did the best he could.

As I got older I started to study Judaism and *Torah* at length. I found in it things I could believe in and never pretended to believe things I didn't. I became active in the local temple mostly to have an excuse to get away from Levi. See he never went to or wanted to go to the local shul because... well he was raised orthodox don't you know and even though he knew next to nothing about Judaism—and nothing at all about *Torah*—he knew "how things should be done." According to him, everything they did at a Reform shul was just wrong. So I could go and sit with people who had known me my whole life—though I rarely saw them. They were really happy to have me because they were a really old congregation and needed new blood. They made me feel like I had a place to belong. When I turned out to be gay they had a hiccup but shortly they just accepted me because—let's face it—they always knew. Then when Liz started coming with me and later converted... well when we got married by a Rabbi they were all there.

So when I say I'm not even going to temple now you know I'm in a really bad way.

I have made my hell right here on earth. It's not God's fault; it wasn't a plan. My life is hell because I can't let go of things, and I can't let go of things because I have PTSD. I have PTSD because people did horrible things to me. If I didn't have PTSD I could probably believe that I didn't deserve to be treated this way. I might understand that the people who did it only did it because they were broken inside. I wouldn't need to have an apology to let me know that I didn't do anything wrong; I would know that I was a victim and I wouldn't still be a victim.

When I was in a good place and had it all figured out no one or nothing could have dragged me back into that pit. If I didn't have PTSD maybe I could just give up.

Maybe I would at least know what it meant.

I have Post-Traumatic Stress Disorder. I'm trying to fix myself. It's hard, but I am determined to get to a place where when I look in the mirror and say "I love you" and I can really mean it. I want to get to a place where when I push my hand into my chest over my heart and say "Good morning, I love you,"—as I was told to do—that I feel love course through me.

I want to feel worthy just because I'm alive.

I want to feel that piece of God that is in me that I felt once and no longer do. I want to know again what I once fully believed—that the piece of God that is my soul is always there for me when I am still and quiet. That it knows what to do even when I don't have a clue.

I want to go and vote and know that my vote counts. I want to work to make that a truth. I want to find a way to make a difference and accept that I do instead of down-playing everything that I do that might have merit because no one else ever says it does—or worse yet not enough people say it.

People have spent a lifetime tearing me down, using and abusing me. I keep trying to get ahead to succeed at something and I never do. I keep building relationships with people who care much less for me than I care for them. I am drawn to those kinds of people because those are the kind of people I have always known. They treat me like crap. I don't think I deserve it, but I must because these are the only people I find. I collect these kinds of people because I don't trust anyone. I especially don't trust anyone who is telling me that goodness, love and light, success and riches are just around the corner—because every time I have been told that, every time I dared to believe it, it has always turned out to be a huge lie.

I make my strongest relationships with people who take and take and never give back because I don't feel worthy of good people's time, I fear that they will see the wrongness of me. When I felt good about myself I drew good people to me and felt accepted and loved, but the Universe didn't let me keep that.

If the human existence is just a classroom for the soul, what am I learning from a lifetime full of being the whipping boy? I am learning nothing of merit from having a crappy life except that if I continue to put myself out there and love people with my whole heart I will continue to be hurt.

If I work hard and persevere I will manage to live to work hard and persevere another day. I am learning that nothing I do really matters and that the only thing I can count on from one day to the next is physical and emotional pain.

My spiritual and emotional wells are dry. Mentally I'm a train wreck. My pain gives me a unique view of the human condition. Most of the time when a friend or family member is having a hard time I seem to know just what to say and do to make them feel better. Maybe that is why my life sucks—so that I can help others by saying the things I need people to say to me, doing for others what I need to have done for me.

The problem is my compassion is broken. I can't put any more into the well of humanity while drawing out nothing. True or not my perception is that there is a lack of balance in my life. The "terrible" is a mountain the "good" is a mole hill.

Since my son started smoking, drinking and doing drugs, the only thing that has brought me true joy has been my grandson. Now they have moved him away and the therapist tells me that I will now be like a regular grandparent instead of a guardian. But that isn't what I want. What I wanted was to know when I was going to have him and for how long so that I could build some semblance of a life as I co-parented him. Instead they just took him with the whole "After all, we *are* his parents" thing. But what about all the time they couldn't bother to be parents or when they wanted to work and changed when I had him every other day?

When you are dealing with someone else's chaos you know what you can't do? You can't live an un-chaotic life. Now you are all saying, "Well now you can." Can I? Because I really *want* to spend real time with my grandson the way I always have, and in order to do that at all I will still have to keep everything open because they aren't going to manage their time any better now than they ever have.

They may win. This move may be just the change Ryan and Jenny need to be the best people they can be. My grandson might be better than fine with the move; he may enjoy having his parents more. But my heart is broken and there can be no big win for me. In this I lose.

If it is better for all of them I can be happy for them, but that won't make me any happier.

I lose what I want, and they get what they want. It is the pattern of my life: I lose; other people win. I keep trying; I keep failing. I keep doing the right thing to the best of my ability; it keeps making me a victim. Loving has led always to heartache. At the end of the day, what has fifty-nine years of life pushing through trauma done for me? A great big nothing. Yet I lack the courage to kill myself.

Today is my son's father's visitation. Why so long after his death? You know... autopsy, police investigation, all the lovely things that go with someone killing themselves in a house where their loved ones are present. And of course there is the getting his family here from the Northeast.

He's left a huge mess for everyone to clean up, and today they will stand around and saint him. He was a horrible person who never had an ounce of regret for any of the people he trampled in his need to be happy at any cost. He never apologized to anyone. He never made amends. Yet today they will lie about how he died and hold him up as a pillar of the community. They will talk about all the lives that were enriched because of him and never once will they talk about all of the people he hurt or ruined. His victim's psyches lie in unmarked graves, yet even in death he has more respect than I have in life because he wasn't a queer—a drug addict and a pervert—but not a queer.

Now this is funny because I am using the gay card a lot lately and I never have before except in very private circles. But my father couldn't stand me because he always knew I was at least a lesbian and most likely transsexual. I'm pretty butch. In truth, have never seen myself as either male or female but something somewhere in the middle leaning heavily towards male.

My father did all the seriously screwed up things he did to me in an effort to stop me from being queer thus driving it into every part of my functioning brain that what I was, always was, was completely wrong. That will fuck you up in ways you can never know unless you went through it.

I pushed past all of the crap once and embraced myself in love. I found communion with my soul. I wasn't "happy," but I was at peace. I was content. Then the shit hit the fan and my PTSD exploded. All of the things I had shoved down for years wouldn't leave me alone. I was an idiot for letting those things happen and now I was looping. The same images, the same thoughts over and over in my head bad enough, but the main thing about PTSD is that it makes you *feel* the same emotions that you felt—the same fear, the same anxiety, the same pain—over and over and over again. It's like an elephant is sitting on your chest; your brain feels like it is on fire. It taints everything you are doing and steals any joy you might have. It beats you with the huge stick of your unworthiness. I had to deal with all these things once and for all. I realized I was out of my league, so I went to therapy where they told me it would get worse before it got better.

They were not wrong.

The whole time I have been dealing with this trying to be better Liz has been completely unhelpful. She wants to help but doesn't know how because she is incapable of not feeling slighted because I am unhappy. "Why is she not enough?" I don't know, maybe she could try to actually get off her ass and do something for me, put me first. How about she could stop snipping at me every time I speak or move?

For once in my screwed up life I need someone to put me first to help me out of the darkness. She can't be that person which has really ruined our marriage. We are now those old people who stay together because they are so used to living together they don't know what else to do.

Does she add anything to my life at this point? She pays the bills and supports me financially, but she has let me down emotionally, and I don't know if that is something that can ever get over. I don't know that it is something that won't be between us from now on—the whole I'm drowning in my own waste she can't put out her hand to help me because some of it might get on her thing.

I need calm and she just keeps yelling at me over bullshit.

And the whole time, every time I almost pulled myself out of the pit, something else horrendous happened and she just keeps yelling about everything because something is eating her and she doesn't care about what's happening to me and so... I don't give a damn about what's happening to her.

Today a room full of people is going to celebrate the long, joy-filled life of the man who abused me. I'm going to die and people will say "she was alright even though she was gay and/or a Jew, she was a hard worker." He is dead at his own hand—a fact they will hide from all his Jesus-jamming friends. He shot himself as a last "fuck you" to everyone he left behind. He never did anything for anyone unless money was involved, and they are even now knocking each other down to talk about what a great guy he was, what a model citizen, how funny and intelligent he was, how enlightened.

He did things to me that have given me nightmares for over forty years. He broke me in ways it is hard to break people and stole my son's love from me as the cherry on the top of the shit pile. You know because I'm the thing that is an abomination.

All those people who pray for his immortal soul today and say how great he was, do they all believe that it's alright for a thirty-four-year-old, twice-divorced man to marry a sixteen-year-old virgin girl, do whatever he wants to her, then take her to a drug den in New York, drug her and then he and his friends think it's a party? Do they believe that it's alright for a man to sleep with his best friend's wife then drug his own wife so that his friend can sleep with her to "even the score?" Because that's what he did to his first wife. He used his next "best friend" to steal from the company that his friend worked for behind his back. Hell, he sold his "friend's" widow's uncle's property—which he didn't even own!

What do they think? They think he accepted Jesus as his lord and savior and that all those black marks are erased from his soul forever. While his victims pay for his crimes. That isn't justice.

Where is my apology, you son of a bitch?! Where is your amends? I forgave him so many times. I had forgiven him again. It was hard but I did it for me and now he has done something to my son. Something to darken forever my son's life, and who does my son blame? He blames *me* because I am always what is wrong. I'm an easy target because I am so different.

"You really aren't you know," I tell myself, looking over my shoulder at what I have just typed.

I spin in my chair to face the cursed apparition.

"What?" I ask me.

"We aren't that different. This is the disconnect in a human's ability to truly living a meaningful, enlightened life—the fact that we see people as "the other." If when people saw me they didn't judge me and find me wanting, I would not judge them and find them wanting—because that is what we do. The minute you get the idea that someone is judging you and finding you wanting you immediately start to look for their faults. They didn't give you a pass, so you just can't give them a pass. Our son is broken; we helped break him. It wasn't a plan. We did the best we could."

"My best was never good enough for anyone," I said. "My best was never good enough because everyone always judged me and found me wanting."

"We can never do better than our best, so our best is *always* good enough, and anyone who says otherwise should just go fuck themselves. If everyone judges us, so the fuck what? That's *them* not *us*. Screw them. Opinions are like assholes; everyone has one. Just give up."

Then of course I was gone again.

"Son of a bitch," I mumbled.

I was different, but I was never authentic till I had been out of the closet for years. When I was authentic... then I had even more enemies than I had friends. Openly gay and living as a Jew I now came under fire from whole groups of people just for living.

Many of you think I give fundamentalist Christians a raw deal. After all, we are all the same, right? I have not said anything as hateful as they do about Jews much less LBGTQ people. They not only hate us, they show up at our funerals with signs that say *God* hates us.

Saying God hates us allows them to do anything they want to us because now treating us like crap is the same in their eyes as serving God. This is what religions—all of them—have always done. They make it "us and them" and then convince themselves that only they serve God. Since they are serving God, what they do and say must be right. That makes everyone else *wrong*. When things are *wrong* you must snuff them out. It only makes sense.

Except that it doesn't.

When you say it out loud you can start to see it for what it is—bullshit. If God really hated people just for being what they are... well why are they here? Why did he make them in the first place? Was it to be sacrificial lambs for the righteous? That's also bullshit.

If God hates me for being gay then why did God make me this way? Why do I exist? Is it only so that the righteous can worship their god by being hateful to me? How does that make them better people? Isn't that what the whole religion thing is supposed to be about—making people the best they can be? It doesn't at all, but that's supposed to be the plan.

I'm trying to work things out. My personal life sucks right now and I'm fighting PTSD as the hits just keep coming. You know what I don't need? Some rich orange ass hat stirring everyone up into a froth of otherness, that's what. He is using the oldest trick in the book—divide and conquer. The worst part is it's working.

How can I deal with all my personal crap when it seems like we are all doomed anyway? My personal problems with my family and money seem infinitesimal compared with climate change beating the crap out of the planet while the dumbass in the White House insists it's not mankind's fault and let's just keep drilling and fracking and making trash. Let's not put any time or money into renewable energy, no, let's burn the candle at both ends and watch it all go up in flames. He is working towards nothing as hard and fast as a nuclear holocaust and stirring the terrorists into a rage while giving them all the opportunity they need to attack us. He is arming home born terrorists with automatic weapons and thirty-round banana clips, and he is doing all those things for one reason. To keep his base. So why does his base want to destroy the plant? Because they are ready for the End of the World; they are ready for Judgement Day because all of *us* will be sent to hell and *they* will all go to heaven.

Like I said, religion is a problem.

I've read so many damn self-help books that I am one of the idiots who has made people rich who say such stupid assed things as, "if you can dream it you can be it." None of those books tell you what to do when you have nothing going for you. In dark times fight for the light, it's the only way to get through it. Fight for the light, rage against the darkness. Be the change you want to see. Just be. All those things sound good, they do, but none of them work unless you have something that you can grab onto that keeps hope alive. We all need something that gives our life meaning. Hanging on to something as unfathomable and untouchable as God to get you through the hard times... well you'd better be good at lying to yourself.

Chapter Eleven

My mother is an amazing woman, quiet, stoic, funny, hardworking. She's seventy-seven and still goes to work five days a week at an office where the work is so stressful that most people start there and quit. She is kind and gentle—and a textbook, classic enabler. Anyone with a penis gets an automatic pass. She gave my dad a pass; he was like living with Doctor Jekyll and Mister Hyde. She enables my twenty-year-old, six-foot two-inch, two-hundred-fifty-pound nephew to sit on his ass all day in her house, eat her groceries, and do... not a fucking thing. She has to come home from work and clean up after him. She made excuses for my father and now she makes excuses for my nephew.

Why?

Because she was taught that men were better than women. You see her father was raised orthodox. Women weren't good enough to read *Torah*, not good enough to study it, and—though she grew up in a Reform shul—in her house growing up her father ruled the roost. She grew up in the South where the kids she went to school with... well their fathers were more misogynistic than hers ever was. They were pretty poor, and their father ate first because he had to work and "needed his energy." The wife and kids ate after he did. In all fundamentalist religions—yours mine everyone else's—women are somewhere far below men. They are supposed to keep to their station and never rise above it. They are taught to enable their men to make excuses for them, to take their abuse and neglect, and give them a pass on their bad behavior because after all they have a penis.

This is not men's fault; it is just the way things are. You see these religions also teach men that their women are beneath them and that it is alright for them to abuse or neglect women, that women are here only to serve men and spit out babies. They can't see that these beliefs stop them from having actual full lives as much as it does their women. They never know what it's like to have an equal partner who can take up the slack and who actually loves them. They have to always be tough and strong and never give in to their own feelings. They get to be king of their kingdom, but it is a sad kingdom full of prisoners.

Why is fundamentalist religion such a haven for sexism, abuse and bigotry? Because it was created by men who wanted power over everyone else and it was perpetuated by priests who needed to keep their phony-baloney jobs.

The leaders of the world early on in the evolution of the human species were always male. They were bigger and stronger than their female counterparts and filled with testosterone which made them both horny and aggressive. Smaller and not as strong, the female of the species needed the protection of the male.

Male dominance is no longer necessary for the survival of the species, and we have evolved past the need of fundamentalist religion to keep us in check. Women don't need men to survive, and fundamentalist religion no longer makes people better. No, fundamentalism is the "defendable" excuse people use for being absolutely the worst people they can be. It is the excuse they use to create "us and them," and "them" often includes half the species.

I hate being a woman, always have, because in my family only men get a pass. Only men had power.

While we are easily offended by bigotry, we are often not as hard on the open sexism we live with in this country every day. For the same job women don't earn the same amount of money as men. There are still jobs women are not allowed to hold even if they are fully capable.

Bigotry didn't occur till one kind of people ran into another kind of people. Even now people who are the "same" don't persecute people in their own races—you know unless you stir in religion. But women... women have always been seen as "less than."

Not just by men, either, many women even now see themselves as less than men. This is the lasting "gift" fundamentalist religion has brought to the species. After all, how can a woman be a "true believer" and not believe that she is less than her husband? She, woman, was an afterthought; she came from his side.

Trump didn't win the popular vote, but he did win the election. How did he do that? He did that by always appealing to his base. What is his base? Evangelical Christians... and only Muslim extremists think less of women than Fundamentalist Christians do.

Of course both would tell you that they love women, but of course women have to understand their place. Unfortunately they do, and they proved it when they voted for Trump. Women who voted for Trump did so for two reasons: first no woman could possibly be president... that's not a woman's place; second they gave him a pass for saying "When you are famous you can grab women by their pussies" even though that is a really unholy thing to think and way to feel because that's "just the way men are" and after all men are better than women.

I believe fundamentalist religion is in its death throes. Human kind is trying very hard to evolve our spirits at least as fast as we have evolved our bodies. We will be fully evolved as a species—if we don't help Trump and his friends destroy the planet before the experiment is completed—when we see everyone as the same. When we don't try to pigeon hole anyone, when we all do exactly what we want the way we want without fear of what other people will think because everyone is way too busy enjoying their own life to try to tell anyone else what they should do with theirs. We will only evolve spiritually when women are equal to men and men are equal to women, when our differences are seen as a blessing not a curse.

I would like to be fully evolved. In my life as a child I saw clearly that men were better than women. My dad made all the rules, we always did what he wanted to do, if you didn't follow the rules there was swift punishment. Even if I wasn't the kind of woman that I am I would have grown up thinking that men were superior to women. Except that isn't exactly correct because I never wanted to be a woman; I just was. If I'm honest, I never thought men were better than women. What I thought was that it was better to be a man. That being a woman meant you could never have the things you wanted or be who you wanted to be because men had all the real power.

Men have all the power because women gave it to them a long time ago in order to survive and now we don't need them to survive they still hang on tight to that power. Right now it is no better to be a man than it is to be a woman because today's man is having trouble figuring out just what his role is. Moving towards equality isn't easy; the people in control never want to give up that power. We were moving steadily towards equality, and so everyone who was super afraid of all these huge changes... They are the Trump base. They are happy with men controlling women and the rich controlling the poor even if they are female and/or poor. They don't want to worry about the environment. They want to cling to the rules the preacher has made for them because then they don't have to choose things for themselves that might land them in hell and they don't dare not to believe in hell because if they don't then... what will happen to all the people they hate at the end of days?

They will happily live out their days in misery because they are that afraid of change. They are afraid that change will destroy the lives they have made—and make no doubt they have worked hard to have the lives they have. The change might make their lives worse. Certainly the Affordable Care Act helped many, but it destroyed the economies of the working poor. It destroyed our "disposable" income so that we now live more or less hand-to-mouth. We couldn't afford it, but we had to have it or pay a fine. It has made the last few years progressively harder for us as we have a little less money each year.

I am afraid of change. I especially hate the change someone else makes for me that doesn't work for me, but I know when there has to be a change. I know it isn't right and could never be good for one group of people to ruin the world to fill their pockets or for one group of people to subjugate another.

My son made a choice for himself that he felt he had to make; it ruined the life I had made for myself. I now have to scramble to try to fill the hole his choice made in my life, but when I'm sane I know he didn't really move just to hurt me. He moved because he needed to make a change to fix his own life. What sucks is that he didn't give even a moment's thought to how it would hurt me or what the move might do to Avy.

To be given something amazing and then have it snatched away that is what will put you in the bottom of the pit. That is the question that never gets answered satisfactorily in those self-help books: what do you do, how do you cope when you lose the thing you care about most? What do you do when everything else sucks, too, and then *Boom!* someone drops the hammer and separates you from who you thought you were?

We tie ourselves to people, places, things. People ask us who we are and we don't answer, "A soul looking for enlightenment who is trying to be kind and loving in the face of diversity." No we answer, "I'm a plumber, I'm a mother, I'm a husband, I'm a wife, I'm a father, I'm a writer or a brick layer, I'm a grandparent, a minister, a Rabbi, I'm President of the United States." But you rarely get to hang on to any title, real or imagined. I can no longer consider myself a writer because my definition of a writer is someone who makes a living writing. What have I done for the last nine years? I have taken care of my grandson. I am a grandmother, but now I don't get to take care of my grandson. In fact, I rarely get to see him at all.

So... what am I! Though I do services at the local temple occasionally I can't call myself a Rabbi because I lack the credentials. I never wanted to be a woman; I am one and I'm fifty-nine, and so it's a little late to take my life in a different direction. I have a small farm, but my goats are in various stages of dying, crops have sucked for years because of climate change, and so I'm no longer a farmer.

In the South being female—much less Jewish and gay—doesn't give me a lot of opportunity for real or lasting friendships. Without my grandson I'm sort of alone most days. All busted up for weeks yet still having to do my chores, I haven't had a whole lot of energy. And of course I get no sympathy because my wife was sick most of the time I've been debilitated and my son's father was busy dying till he shot himself—making him a big-time hero.

It's a lot to deal with, and I want to be the one to answer the question of "How do I hold onto my spirituality in difficult times? How do I get through times of great suckage?" I want to answer it because I want to know, and mostly what I get when I delve into the many books I have around here is that basically I have to imagine that things are better. That I do have control and that I can make my life better. All I have to do is let go of the hateful past, be present, and imagine that things are going to get better. All I have to do is be present in this moment. After all, the past can't be changed, and the future is an illusion.

My pain—is that an illusion, too? If so, can I wish it into the corn field? What about my anxiety and my feeling that I will never be happy again? I have all those things right now in the wonderful present moment. This moment and the present moments of the last couple of months have been filled with physical and emotional pain. Grief at what I have lost. Loneliness, anxiety, hopelessness—these are my constant companions.

That is what I have at this present moment, and when I try to focus on this present moment you know what always comes up? That I would be waiting for my grandson to get off the bus, or putting him in bed for the night, reading him a story, or playing some game with him. That I'd be laughing with him or making him dinner, or a dozen other things that I have gotten used to doing over the years, things that became part of my routine that have been replace by... nothing, nothing at all. In the "present" everything I do seems like just going through the motions. I get by working myself into a comma or numbing myself out watching tube.

So I'm not "present" because when I stand here in the present with my truth, my life feels pointless, meaningless, empty. I feel hollowed out because my existence is without meaning.

"You're doing it again," she/I say.

This time I was sitting on my porch in the cold minding my own fucking business and I just showed up right in front of me.

"What, what am I doing again!?"

"You are digging the very pit you are in even deeper."

"Now you sound like my fucking wife."

"Where do you think I heard it? That doesn't make it any less true. Why don't you try not thinking about everything that's wrong or could go wrong?"

"You know what would be helpful? Tell me that something great is going to happen in the future. Tell me I'm seconds away from a great big happy event."

"But you're not, what's going to happen if you don't let go is you're going to die young."

"I'm not young now, dumbass."

"You are if you don't die young. If you die young then you aren't young now."

"A pretty sunrise or set, the sun on my face, a handsome tree, a cat's fucking smile, none of those things can pull me out of the pit. People who think they can have never actually experienced true despair."

"Wow, you paid for a full day on the pity train didn't you?"

I got up and stormed in the house as well as my banged-up legs would let me, throwing over my shoulder, "Wow! I never realized I was such a dick!"

"Things just aren't all that bad."

"And see? That just scares the crap out of me that things are going to get even worse. Look I know it could be worse. For the love of God I know things could always be worse! I live in constant fear that things are going to be worse because every time I have ever relaxed even a little bit something horrible happened. Then it's me on my own scrambling, trying to fix it, and telling myself that things will be good again. I just keep coming out swinging, and life keeps kicking my ass. What is the point of getting off the floor if someone is just going to knock you down? If you can't win why keep trying?"

"What's crazy... and you are fucking crazy you aren't wrong about that. What's crazy is that you can't see that we are winning all the time. Just give up."

She/I was of course gone again.

What did I mean "winning?" I'd never won at anything in my whole crappy life. Oh that's right it's not about living. Well alright what the fuck is it about? Existing? Running out the clock? What's the fucking point of it all? Of anything?

What am I? What is my fucking purpose? Why should I keep going? How do I give up and still keep going? What is the point of trying to do anything if I am just going to move from one failure to another to another?

I did a better job raising my grandson than I did raising my son because I knew better. But how much of the wonderful person he is will stick when he's not with us half the time, when he's with the psycho mom-thing twenty-four/seven or the people she chooses to leave him with? I have run out of hope that she will change for the better. She is narcissistic, and I know way too much about narcissistic people to think she will ever change. Their biggest delusion is that they are, after all, perfect. It is the rest of us who are fucked up. So what have I really accomplished? I was "present" when I was with Avy—always have been and being with him made me as happy as I have ever been—but I had to worry about him whenever he wasn't with me. I had to worry constantly that they would do what they have done and take him away from me. And a better, more put-together person would say he's old enough to take care of himself now, and I took care of him and got to love him when he most needed me. I should just be happy that I made his life a little better for the first part of his life, and maybe it will be enough to break the cycle that made my father, me, and my son so fucking dysfunctional.

Aside from treating me like crap—which is hard to overlook—my son seems to be doing better in every way. He's always been a decent father even when he was on drugs, but now he's apparently doing a really good job. I should just be happy with that.

I would like to be that put-together; I really would, but I miss my grandson. I miss the life I built with him in it. I miss all our little rituals and routines, the things that made me feel like I was important and loved.

What do I do now? I have nothing. The only reason I have to get up in the morning is to take care of livestock, and my goats are dying now, so what is the real point of that?

Olivia was busy putting things into her computer. She had just told me all about what to expect with the EMDR. Once again I was warned that things could get worse before they got better. I just don't think anyone—even Olivia—understood that if it got any worse I just couldn't take it.

She wasn't asking me any more questions, so I just started talking.

"What do I do that has worth? I'm sad and alone. How do I fix that? I have pulled myself through a river of crap many times and kept going, but this feels like it is too much.

"I miss Avy. I miss the relationship I once had with Ryan. We have a horrible relationship now which is obvious from what I've already said. Here's the thing: I can't fix my relationship with him because the one thing I cannot be in his presence is me. I can't be authentic when I'm with him because I have to act like all his choices are good ones. I have to kiss his ass and Jenny's, too, or I will never get to see my grandson at all. Ryan baits me—so does his wife—and I have to bite my tongue and nod. It gives them a feeling of ultimate power and makes them feel good about who they are to 'put me in my place.'

"What sort of person must I be that I can never be myself around anyone else? I live in pieces. A piece of me I can share with this one and another piece with that one, but I can never be all of me because my obvious wrongness already makes people uncomfortable. Some of the people I love best... they voted for Trump because they hated Hillary that much. Why did they hate Hillary? When you hear their bullshit reasons you know why—because she didn't have a penis. Male and female, my friends who voted for Trump or—just as bad—threw their vote away on a third party candidate really did so because Hillary was a woman. They will tell you they love you then vote for someone who would like to put you and everyone like you on a boat in the ocean with a hole in it and a teaspoon to bail with."

"Wow! You're jumping all over the place today. Are you this worried about having the EMDR therapy?" Olivia is nothing if not observant.

I thought about it before I blurted out an answer. I took a deep breath, let it out and answered.

"What if I do this and it doesn't work either? What if I do this and I'm just as fucked up as I am right now?"

"What if you do it and you are healed? Let yourself think about that."

Yeah, that will work.

Good people, worthwhile people learn the power of a real apology. They learn that in order not to make the same bad mistakes over and over again they have to recognize the fact that they screwed up and own it. How can you look at what is happening to our country and still defend that you voted for Trump? How do you think your ethnic friends feel about the way you voted? What about your friends that would like to leave their children and grandchildren something other than a smoldering hole? Do you think they understand your position that Hillary would have been worse?

For the record, we don't think anyone—except maybe Ted Cruise—would have been worse. We see what you did with your vote at the best was you picking a side and sticking to it no matter what, and at worse we see you as only slightly less treasonous, raciest and sexist than Trump is.

People my age remember the Civil Rights Movement. In our lifetime people were treated like second-class citizens, ripped from their homes, and hung at the whim of white Christians filled with hate because those people wanted to be treated... well, like *people*.

Christians don't apologize for slavery or the Jim Crow South, any more than they apologize for the Crusades, the rape of North and South America, the Inquisition or the Holocaust, even though *all* of those things were carried out proudly by Christian people. Yet they want all Muslims to admit to being terrorists.

All Muslims are not terrorists any more than all Christians are as full of hate as the fundies are.

There were and are Christians who have denounced all those atrocities and even those who have apologized. Just as there are many moderate Muslims who have stood against terrorism and injustice even though to do so makes them a target of radicalized Muslim extremists.

Most know what they have done personally and feel blameless. They don't speak up against the atrocities of their individual groups because to do so is to admit to wrong doing. They can't defend the actions of their peers, and don't want to be painted with the same brush, and yet that is exactly what *they* do.

All Gays, Jews, Blacks, Hispanics, Christians, Whites, Asians, Muslims, Straights, Arabs, all people who drive a Prius, do XYZ. That's the problem—people assuming what other people are based on a stereotype. People assuming because one Muslim screams that he hates Jews, Christians, all Americans, that they all do. When you see footage of blacks in the sixties doing nonviolent protest as whites spit on them, beat them, and set their buses on fire—often with help from the police—we could say all fundamentalist Southern Christians are raciest haters.

We were raised that way; we had to learn better. If blacks hadn't risen up and integrated, that hate would still be there. We are seeing now that some of that hate still runs deep, and where is it hiding? In the churches and homes of those people who consider themselves the most beloved of God.

That's always where bitter hatred thrives, where it is cloaked in religious belief. God wants us to own, rape, kill you because you aren't human. We are better than you are; you are what's wrong because you don't pray the same way we do.

Hell I was a homophobe. I knew I was queer my whole life, yet there was no one who ever said any more hateful things about homosexuals than I did in my youth.

Why? Because I "believed" that it was evil. It was hard to let go of what I "believed" about myself and embrace what I knew to be true. I said the things I said and believed what I believed because that was what I was told the way I was programed. I was a homophobe because I knew I was gay, and if I had to live my life in a lie because it was the "right" thing to do, everyone else should, too. After all it was against God to be queer. Everyone said so, and there were no gay role models when I was a kid, none. No one in my life was telling me it was alright to be what I knew I was—quite the opposite.

Why do people have such blind hate? Because if I point my finger at others maybe no one will notice that I don't make the cut. As long as I am picking on "the other," maybe they won't notice the wrongness of me and they will leave me alone or better yet near worship me because I stand for something.

Humanity sucks ass.

"I actually think that shows real progress," Olivia said.

"Really? Because it doesn't seem like progress to me, it feels like I'm the world's biggest throw rug."

I left her office not feeling like I was progressing at all. And apparently the real reason she was waiting to do the EMDR therapy was because neither the equipment she needed to do it nor her paperwork had come in. In fact, the equipment had been backordered. That kind of tells you what my life is like in a nutshell right there.

Why did she think I was making "progress?" My friend Jason just left. By the time he finally did, it took all my resolve and self-control to keep from telling him off and maybe strangling him in his sleep. He stayed with us for three weeks—in the room where we know there are no bugs. I don't guess I'm ever going to be really sure about the rest of this damn house. Thanks, God.

During the whole time Jason stayed with us he tried to "fix" me by telling me over and over that I wasn't really depressed and had nothing to be depressed about. I had everything I really needed and just needed to change my perspective.

Here's a little perspective for you. Why was Jason at our house for three weeks? Because after years of supporting his whiney, maudlin, depressed ass—he did nothing but mess up their home and spend his husband's money—Jeff had finally had enough and he kicked Jason out. So Jason was basically living in his car and in the home of any friend he could mooch off for a few weeks till he got tired of their pedestrian food, atmosphere and or way of thinking. Then he moved on to greener pastures. You see Jason... he's very "edgy."

He was at one time a fairly successful sculptor, but... you know his very real depression—not the fake-ass shit I have—kept him from creating. Now he goes from house to house telling his friends that all their problems are made up and they just have to let go the way he has.

Here is the speech I didn't give him that I wanted to and that my therapist told me I was doing a good job because I didn't tell him this and/or wring his fucking hypocritical throat... "Hey there, too cool for school, one of us has their dead-beat friend sleeping in their paid-for house, eating all the groceries they raised, and the other one is basically living in their fucking car. At the end of the day I hope I am remembered as being kind not edgy because you see, being edgy—I can't help that. I don't work at being weird; I just am. But being kind is a practice; it's something I work hard at. So now you need to get your lazy, self-righteous, inauthentic ass right up out of my house."

Of course I didn't have to give that speech because right before I was losing it and ready to just let fire with both verbal barrels we ran out of the "good" cheese, and he moved on to those greener pastures… You know, Larry and Barbara's house. They have called three times in the last two days; he is already driving them fucking crazy so… Maybe my shrink is right and I'm making progress.

Now why did I say Jason is inauthentic? (The other things are after all explained in the story I just told about him.) Because he *works* at being "edgy"… he isn't. He's actually a fairly normal guy who is always pretending. He is really a nice guy, but he is so afraid of being seen as "pedestrian" that he goes out of his way to do weird shit. Case in point: Jeff once said he didn't even think Jason was actually gay that he was just screwing guys because it gave him an oddball credit. He drank too much, smoked too much weed, ate ludes like candy, and then wouldn't eat anything that was "bad for his temple." He could sculpt anything but spent a year sculpting nothing but animals that looked like penises and of course when these didn't sell… well that was what caused the depression "the real depression"—once again nothing like the "fake" shit I'm going through.

He used to be a really neat guy, but when he started to make it as an artist… well he was the first one that bought his brand and since then he has become ever phonier. I'm not sure what his real voice is anymore, and I'm sure he has no clue.

He's always putting on a fucking act, but the less he is his real self, the less people care about the person he is pretending to be… or his art.

I need to thank him because I think maybe that's a lesson I needed to learn. Maybe as long as I continue to be me I'm not as bad off as I think I am, so… Maybe he's right about my depression.

Olivia looks confused then says, "I'm not sure I understand what you mean."

I go back over what I've just said, *I have to forgive in order to heal, but they won't let me forgive them.*

"Forgiveness is a gift we give ourselves that's what they all say."

"Who are 'they'?"

"All the spiritual gurus that write the books that make them rich and then nothing they say has any real meaning because after all they didn't fail at life. You can't forgive someone when they don't apologize.

"The victim of a great wrong stays a victim as long as they hide what happened, and why do we do that? Because we are afraid no one will believe us—or worse yet—that they will believe us but will make excuses for the people who have hurt us. We're most afraid they may tell us it was alright for this person to do what they did to us. I'm having trouble moving from being a victim to a survivor because everyone always makes excuses for the people who did horrible things to me. My mother makes excuses for my dad and Levi never admitted to much less was sorry for anything he did to me. He always had a reason. He always found a way to blame me for the horrible way he treated me. That makes me feel like the perpetual victim. If anyone who had ever wronged me would have admitted to what they had done and said they were truly sorry, then the healing might have begun immediately.

"If my mother would just once admit the way my father treated me—and her for that matter—I might be able to let go of my pain. She won't do it. I love her, but she has never had my back—ever.

"If my abusers had admitted to their crimes against me it would have released me from my wrong-thinking that the horrible things they did to me are somehow my own fault."

"But you know now, don't you, that it is never the victim's fault that they are victimized? That you don't own any of the wrong that was done to you; it was all them. It was the things that were broken in them, never that there was anything wrong with you, right?"

She is careful when she asks her questions, which is how it should be, but if I'm honest I am always careful in how I answer them, too. I'm not at all sure if that is what I should be doing, but... well I'm pretty sure she would be remiss in her responsibilities if she didn't have me locked up if I said what I really thought sometimes. But I mostly say what I'm thinking in there because otherwise, what's the point?

"When people don't own the wrong they have done, when they don't apologize, they ask their victim to suffer through what was done to them over and over again. I am the only one who is punished for the crimes others committed against me. My dad... he at least wanted to be a better person. He at least worked at it, and I think his own thoughts tortured him more than anything anyone could have done to him. As bad as some of the things he did were... well I really believe he was doing the best he could because... well I fucked up Ryan and I know I was doing the best I could do. The difference is I apologized to my son, but my father never apologized to me.

"I needed him to say he was sorry for the way he treated me. All he ever did was tell me that it never happened or worse yet that it was my fault. But I forgive him, I can forgive him because I think he did feel bad for what he did to me, the way he treated me, he just couldn't say it. That may be bullshit but if so it's bullshit that makes me feel better, so who cares.

But Levi... That bastard delighted in nothing as much as making other people squirm, in abusing mankind, in using people and scamming them then laughing about it because they looked stupid. He made fun of them because they had ever for one minute trusted him. He was a *gonif*. I'm trying, but I can't forgive him because his dying act was not one of owning any of the evil he had done and being repentant. No, his last act was

139

instead a giant fuck you to everyone and maybe mostly to Ryan, but Ryan hates me."

"What did you need from Levi?"

"I needed him to admit to what he did. Tell me exactly what had been done to me so that I no longer have to deal with the shadows of that moment. I needed him to just once feel my pain. Feel the pain of all the people he hurt. Instead at the moment he started to have physical pain he killed himself. He died and never paid for anything, nothing. I am paying for the crimes he committed against me, and my son is paying for the evil his father did to him, and yet I am the villain in Ryan's story. I don't believe in hell, but I live there."

"I think the EMDR therapy will help take you out of hell. Here's your exercise for this week. Every time you start to think about Levi I want you to say, 'I didn't deserve to be treated that way' till the thoughts go away."

I tried it; it almost worked. Then I had to annualize why it was working, and that just talked me right out of it—which just proved to me that not even my therapist understood how screwed up my brain was.

Sometimes there really are two sides to a story. If you choose for instance to scream in someone's face and maybe shove them, they punch you in the head and lay you out—you own part of that. It is not all your fault nor is it all theirs; it is two people acting like assholes and losing their tempers in different ways. I might do something that offends you, or you might do something that offends me, and if it is not my intention or yours to offend it is a simple misunderstanding. Under these conditions—and only these—is it alright to defend your actions in an apology.

If you are acting towards me with violence screaming in my face or shoving me I will hit you before I have a chance to think about it. If you didn't want me to punch you in the face you maybe should have thought about how you were acting. Knowing that I have a violent streak I should have walked away before the fight got that far. We are both wrong.

Here is the real rub: my logical mind knows what is right and how to do it, but my emotional mind—my ego—often gets in the way of me doing the right thing—not for others but always for myself.

If you say or do something that offends me I have not actually been injured. I shouldn't assume that it's about me; I should tell you what made me uncomfortable—make sure you don't think I'm just joking with you—and then accept your apology that starts, "It was not my intention to offend you…"

You can't be held accountable for what I might be offended by if you don't know me well enough to know. A joke is a joke. If I do not clearly tell you how I feel, why I feel that way, and give you the opportunity to explain yourself, then I don't then have the right to try to destroy you and all you care about because of my perception that I was somehow abused.

You know who never makes an assumption that they have been physically or sexually assaulted? Those of us who have been actually physically and/or sexually assaulted, that's who. If you are wondering whether you have or have not been damaged, the answer is you have not. Don't "Me, too" with your story that you willingly went home with a man, had consensual sex with him, but in the middle decided you didn't want to do it and he didn't pick up on your nonverbal cues.

You were not sexually assaulted. What you did was make a mistake and you had bad sex. Last time I looked being bad in bed wasn't a crime, and having consensual sex and being disappointed didn't make someone a victim. In that scenario you're a victim of nothing but your own bad judgement. What you are doing by telling a story such as that is helping to slow the momentum womankind has been making to stop real offenders. People who really do abuse other people should be made to come to terms with what they have done.

In the middle of my meltdown I got "Me, too-ed" by some jackass I was on a panel with at a sci-fi con months before that because I did a joke he didn't like. He accused me of grabbing his leg inappropriately. He wrote a huge rant on his blog about it. Then someone super rich and famous—who was supposed to be my friend—linked to his three-page rant about my "bad behavior" on the panel with her fifteen-page rant about how unprofessionally writers behaved at conventions, and *Boom!* just like that I went from hardly any career to none at all. Thanks, friend. I am drugged and used for group sex at sixteen and no one is punished for it. I do a bad joke and I'm picked to death by virtual piranhas on line.

I'm sorry he was offended; it wasn't my intention. That was the apology I gave that started his followers' feeding frenzy.

And everything else in my life sucks so much that this latest thing just sticks that last nail in the coffin of my sanity.

Here's some advice for real abusive fuckers—don't die without ever admitting to much less apologizing for what you have done. When you do you leave your victim to try to move from victim to survivor on their own. I am paying over and over for a crime Levi and his friends committed. Will anything at all happen to him in the hereafter because of that? I'd like to say yes. I'd like to say Karma will bite him right on the ass, but I don't know that. I certainly have never seen Karma bite the ass of any of my abusers. In fact, if I'm honest, the people who have done the worst things to me who did them only for their own pleasure and greed—it seems that they have been rewarded. They get exactly what they want.

I do a joke, pat a guy on the leg, and I am fried in the court of public opinion. But Levi dies a hero.

I don't have what I want. I should just want what I have, but I can't. I can't because I am filled with bitterness and rage and feel abandoned by God, and why is that? Because no one has ever said, "I'm sorry. That horrible thing that gives you nightmares and makes you wish you were dead so you never had to think about it even one more time—I never should have done that. I was wrong, and I wish I could make it up to you, but I know I can't. It wasn't your fault. It was all me. Please forgive me."

I have to apologize for a joke and am attacked because my apology was "inauthentic." It costs me money and any shred of respect people had for me, but what was done to me... no one has to pay.

You want an authentic apology? Here you go, you Twitterverse asshole. "I'm sorry that you are such a cry bully that you can't let a joke slide. I'm sorry that you hold a grudge for months and then fry me on the world-wide web because you lack the balls to say; *Hey you offended me*, so that I could then apologize. I'm sorry that you are the kind of person who thinks it's alright to crucify someone and ruin their name and their piss-poor career because you can't take a fucking joke—that by the way wasn't aimed at you or anyone else. It was just a fucking joke, you little whining jackass." Now there is your authentic fucking apology. As for my "friend" who used his drivel to make sure I could never make any money at all writing, fuck you, too.

You know what kind of person has to work to be offended? The kind of person who has never had a single bad thing happen to them, that's who.

I'm soaking in the karmic debt of my abusers. Every vindictive, selfish, greed-driven thing people do that hurts another person—their victim carries it with them. It haunts them. It is the shadow that catches in the corner of their eye, the darkness that follows them and won't ever let them fully enjoy the light. You can make all the excuses for your behavior that you want to make; it will not fix them. If you lie to yourself well enough, the evil you have left in your wake... you will never feel guilty about it. But your victim will. They will wonder what it is about them that is so wrong that you would do these things to them. They will wonder why you don't have guilt for the crimes you have committed because *they* have guilt because of what you did.

Having that guy "Me, too" me and having his friends all attack me—it made me feel like I was being raped all over again. I was trying my damndest to put that stuff into a part of my brain where I could deal with it, and this guy ripped the tattered band aid completely off of it. But *I'm* the bad guy.

If someone is a lost cause, it never occurs to them that they should apologize to their victims. But if they have a soul at all the evil they cast trying to have the things they wanted, to be happy "no matter what it did" to other people, it also gives them nightmares, it is also the shadow they see in the corner of their eye. Levi never was tortured like that. He made up an excuse about every bad thing he ever did, and he blamed others for what he alone did. He never paid, nor do I believe he is paying now or will ever pay. I have to fix myself by myself.

I apologized to my son many times. I gave him scars similar but different from mine. He uses my apologies against me. He reminds me of the times I lost my mind and screamed at him. He drags me through how that made him feel, but... at least I released him from thinking it was ever his fault.

We all damage our children and usually in the same but different ways that our parents damaged us because—as wrong as we might know it was—it was what we were taught. When everything in our life is cool and on track we do the best we can not to do what our parents did that screwed us up, but things rarely stay good. When everything goes wrong all it takes is a kid saying something hateful or doing something they know they aren't supposed to do and in our brain something yells, "this is happening because you don't spank him, or yell at him," and before you know it, you are doing the thing you hated most when you were a kid.

You see we want so much for our children, and sometimes—maybe most of the time—the thing that we most want for them is that they not be us, that they don't make the mistakes that we made that screwed up our own lives. When we see them turning into us... it's often more than we can take.

Chapter Twelve

Neither the equipment nor the paper work has arrived so that I can have the EMDR therapy. I am way ready to do it and have it work. I'm at the very end of my rope. No, fuck that, I've already fallen and gone splat on the ground.

"What is the difference?" Olivia asks.

"Academic excellence means someone has achieved knowledge. But academic accomplishment makes it sound like just the knowledge is an accomplishment."

"And you don't believe it is?"

"No, not at all. Learning something—even knowing it—isn't by itself an accomplishment. It's what you do with the knowledge that makes it have worth. You went to school to become a therapist, but if instead you laid brick for a living, just your education wouldn't be an actual accomplishment."

"Alright, now I see your point, but why does it annoy you?"

"Because people who go to college forever think they are better than people like me who only went to the school of hard knocks—even though I graduated with an extension ladder. They spend a fortune to get letters before or after their names and then act like that makes them better than everyone who sweats for a living. Academics are always the first people to put me in my place—you know, somewhere way beneath them—and the first ones to call when something breaks in their fucking house that of course they have no idea how to fix. They know I used to work in construction, so they will call me begging me to fix whatever is broken. Then because I can do it—especially if I can do it quickly—my time is worth nothing and they never want to pay me for anything I do. I should just do it as a fucking favor. What they know they should get paid out the ass for even if they don't use half of what they went to college to learn, but what I have learned in a lifetime of hard work and sweat—something that they could never in a million years do... well that is worth a free beer and a pat on the head. And as you know, I can no longer drink the beer."

Olivia sighs. "Just say no, you won't do it, or tell them up front that you expect to be paid for your time."

"But... it's mostly my friggin' in-laws."

"So the same people who barely tolerate you in their space because they don't like that you are married to their family member."

"Exactly."

"Just tell them no."

That is always easier said than done.

The other day just for a second, for no reason at all, I felt just like I did when I had things all figured out. I didn't feel like a huge, bleeding wound walking around. I was alright with being me; I was alright with my wife being her. I was alright with my life. I didn't want to annualize it; I just wanted to enjoy it. I even told my wife I felt good and didn't want to annualize it to death.

That night I had a great dream. I was important, people all wanted to be with me, talk to me, spend time with me, and in the dream the biggest problem I had was making sure that everyone got to see me as much as they wanted to. The colors in the dream were brilliant. I could smell the foods and drinks; mostly I could feel everyone's love and respect. I usually have many more nightmares than I do good dreams, and often when I have such a great dream it can make me feel far worse when I wake up than a bad dream does. You see when I have a nightmare being awake realizing that isn't real gives me great comfort, but when I have such an awesome dream and wake up to my own life I'm immediately in deep grief over the dream life I had. But this time I was just happy to have had such a great dream. This time the way the dream made me feel stayed with me. That feeling of love and respect I kept it for most of the day.

Of course I had to annualize it. What had happened? Why did I feel better? Why do I feel better? Hell they just shut the government down. My Facebook account was still full of hate mail from the jackass's fans. I wasn't reading any of it, but it was there. I saw what it was and deleted it. My son still isn't really speaking to me. I know because I went to get Avy and Ryan said hi and bye and that was it. But it does look like I will be able to see my grandson. It won't be what it was, but I will still get to spend time with him. Maybe knowing that is why I feel better. Maybe I am just settling into the new crap, getting used to the new wave of not-what-I-wanted but what-I-can-get. Maybe it is just the knowledge that I might get the EMDR therapy soon and it might help. Hel,l at the time I started to feel emotionally, mentally, and spiritually better, I was actually in the middle of a bad cold.

Was it something my therapist said when I saw her two days before? No, when I thought about that I remembered that she asked me if she thought my sessions were helping at all. After all, it was my two year therapy anniversary. She said she thought I had made some progress. I told her I felt like crap but that maybe without therapy I'd be worse. I told her it was like when you have a headache and you take aspirin. Even if your headache doesn't go away you just keep taking the aspirin because if it was that bad when you were taking it just think how bad it would be if you weren't. When I had annualized her question later I decided she was saying that she felt like I was a waste of her time.

So what? What was making me feel better? God knows there hasn't been an inflow of cash and money is still super tight. Thanks to the jackass and my "dear friend" I had NO book sales. My son hasn't showed up out of the blue to say he loves and respects me. This is still the only thing I feel moved to write. The weather has been horrible. My goats are still sick; in fact, the one who was asymptomatic started showing her first hard core symptoms of CAE—swelling in her knees.

But I feel like I'm getting better, why? Did I finally give up? But no, I still didn't know what that meant. Was it because I hadn't had a conversation with myself in a while or had the other me gone away because she was—after all—a figment of my fucked-up imagination and I felt better?

Maybe it was because I realized I'm old and no one expects anything of me. No one cares about anything I do or do not do. At this point in time if I accomplished nothing but existing for the rest of my life no one would judge me. If they did, why would I care? Lots of people younger than I am sit on their asses and do nothing all day, and most of them get a pass.

I don't have any laurels to rest on because I never succeeded at anything, but you know what? No one expects someone to set the world on fire at fifty-nine. All I have to do at this point from now on is just fade away. I can remember me and the friends of my youth saying, "It's better to burn up than fade away." Here's the truth: you'll burn up and then... you'll still have to fade away.

As a youngster I worked hard all the time and... I still work hard all the time. If I had back all the time, energy, and money that I spent doing things for other people—for which I was never paid and was never really even appreciated—I'd be in far better health and have finished so much more for myself. But you see I never felt worthy, so just doing things for myself never seemed good enough. I never thought anyone would like me just for me, so I was always volunteering to help people do things often before they could even ask for my help.

You know the whole "if I can't make you love me I will make you need me" which was taken to the tenth power with my son and wasn't seen as help by him—just as me meddling in his life.

The love you have to buy will never be worth what you paid for it. I don't buy my friends and family things, but I'm the first one there any time they need help with anything. I rarely gave them money because I rarely had enough money that I could afford to lose any. Most of the money I gave people over the years to help them out, it didn't come back and... when I need someone no one ever shows up and volunteers to help me. So what have I learned? Only help people because you want to help. Understand that they will not appreciate your time, your money, or your energy. Know that when people need help it makes them afraid. Then when you help them they feel like they owe you, but they don't want to so... they have to discount your help. They have to make it a favor they did for you to let you help instead of what it is—you giving them a piece of your life that you aren't ever going to get back. So the trick is to only help people if it's what you want to do, if you are enjoying the process of helping them and are expecting nothing in return.

But like I said, that's easier said than done.

I was always running to my son's rescue because I wanted him and my grandson to have a better life. But with rare exception the things I did for him... they were important to me not him. They were things I wanted for him, not things he actually wanted done. He always found the time and money to do the things he wanted to do. He never cared about the things I care about or want for himself the things I wanted for him. I wanted the things I wanted for him because I wanted him to have a better life than I did.

What did he want? To spit on everything that I am. For me to back off and let him do what he wanted to do without judgement. He took all his money and effort and did things I either didn't want him to do at all or things that had no merit to me. I kept trying to give him the best life I could; he kept running from it. I kept trying to save him from failure; he kept running towards it as fast as he could. Even when he would *ask* for my help he never really saw it as help and he still resented it. I *owed* him. I owed him because I once screamed mean things at him and spanked him.

Every bad thing I did to him he has done it to me twenty times over.

And of course this line of thought drove the happy, contented, alright with my world thoughts right out of my head. I of course then had to annualize this. Why? Because my son was still barely talking to me but had made it clear that he was really mad at me for something and I knew eventually we were going to have a talk that I didn't want to have. A talk that was going to make him feel better but me feel worse.

I couldn't afford to feel worse. It was like I had gotten up just to fall further down.

My son walked away from his house and all his things to get a new house and change his life to get away from me because he thinks I am his biggest problem. When I walked around my son's old place—his old house—what did I find? Hours of my hard work, all the things I built him or fixed trying to make him happy. A giant waste of my time and energy because I never succeeded in doing anything that actually helped him. All I did was enable him to continue to do self-destructive things to his life.

He wants someone to blame and I'm an easy target because after all I have always blamed myself for everything. It's super easy for him to make me feel bad, and once I feel bad he can feel good. Human nature doesn't often make any actual sense now does it?

I didn't fail my father. I was gay; he didn't know what to do with a gay kid. He did his best but he failed me, not because there was ever anything wrong with me but because he thought there was. I didn't fail my son. Could I have been a better mother? Yes. Could I have done it then? No. I did the best job I could do at the time. I am much better with my grandson because I know better now. My son chose to do drugs. He made a mess of his life and created a giant hole in mine. I didn't fail him. My choices affected him; the same can be said of any parent. I didn't fail him; he failed me, and he did so because—like my father—he always believed there was something wrong with me. Mostly because it was embarrassing to have a gay mother.

There isn't anything wrong with me.

If I say that a million times will it undo all the times I was told and the many ways I was shown the wrongness of me?

I think I could cut everyone else a little slack if I didn't waste so much time weighing their wrongness against mine. There is nothing wrong with me and there is nothing wrong with them. My son made different mistakes than I made. He's had different traumas. He has taken a different path, and so his conclusions are different than mine. That doesn't make one of us right and the other wrong; it means we think differently because we are different people.

And maybe—just maybe—that's the hardest thing for us to grasp as a parent: that our children aren't us, that they aren't a mere reflection of us or our parenting. They are a combination of all their life experiences, and not every mistake they make will be our fault. Some of them will be all their own damn fault. We just aren't that important to them once they become teenagers. They don't listen to a fucking thing you say, so how can all their problems be our fault?

God has not abandoned me; that is my perception. God loves me but doesn't care what happens to me. The part of me that is connected to the source—my soul—wants me to love myself. My soul knows there is nothing wrong with me. My soul knows that I am the way I am for a reason. Maybe I will never know what that reason is. Maybe I have already done what I am here to do. Maybe something I did or said or wrote helped someone who will do grand things and my only purpose was to help them be the best person they can be.

Maybe when I am long dead people will say, "That guy who slammed Brenda Gold on the internet was a complete cry bully douchebag. She is brilliant!" And my work will have a cult-type following.

Once in a drug-induced, daughter-in-law inspired rage my son yelled at me that, "Nothing you do is important! Nothing!" Now of course he never apologized for that or any of the other horrible things he said that night or over the years, but that's the one I keep going back to. That's the one that stings the most. When I was at his abandoned home and property looking at all the things I had built for him that all lay in various states of decay I realized he didn't just say that; he believes it.

How am I supposed to cope with the knowledge that my son truly believes that nothing I do is important when seeing the decay left in his wake I realized he is right? Nothing I do is important... not even to me.

That's what I have to change. I have to do something—anything—that is important to me. But what?

Here's the problem with the "right now." In the "right now" I only know what has never worked, what will not work. I know what is a waste of time, what has little or no merit, and what just flat sucks. What I don't know, have no idea about, is what I should *do* now. I know I need to do something, but what?

When I was doing all those things at his house what I was really doing was trying to fix problems that couldn't really be fixed by me. But at least while I was doing them I felt like I was helping. In those moments I felt like I could actually make a difference.

I know better now. What wore me out was that no matter what I did for them nothing ever worked the way I thought it would in my head. It never fixed any of the problems between me and my son, and it certainly never fixed anything for them.

There was never anything I could do to save him from himself or from her. It was like the therapist at his rehab told me; I was doing nothing but enabling him. I wasn't bailing him out of jail or giving him money, but I WAS enabling him. I was taking care of things he should have taken care of. Doing things he should have done—all things he could have done if he wanted to but he didn't want to because all he wanted to do was drugs. Drugs own a drug addict. The drugs numb them and make them feel good about themselves. It masks their pain at least for a little while. The horrible way they feel about themselves and life can't break in when they are drunk or stoned out of their gourd.

He is not like me. He rejects everything that I am, everything I think, everything I believe. In fact, I don't dare to have an opinion about anything because he will take an opposite one just for spite.

So what! That doesn't make him right nor does it make me wrong. There is nothing at all wrong with me. I do the best I can, always have. I am working, always am, at being better, trying to understand myself and others. I get knocked down; I get up again.

Except this time.

I can't seem to get to a point where I stop kicking myself as long as other people are kicking me. I just can't. I can say there is nothing wrong with me but as long as people are screaming in my face that I'm what's wrong in the world how can I convince myself that I'm not? I must be what's wrong, right?

Maybe my son's life is going to work out alright after all. Maybe this time THIS new change he feels like he just has to make will be the one that makes him happy. All the drugs and the crazy women, fancy cars and trucks and motorcycles and kids—none of that made him happy. None of that made him even grow up, but maybe this time he's found the magic key to happiness. Maybe I need to work on being alright if he is never happy. Maybe I need to find a way to stop attaching my happiness to other people's. Maybe it's alright for me to be happy even if other people aren't happy with me.

Well they did it. I have no idea where Jenny found them or if she was just doing it to spite me or because they needed to rent the place and this was all they could find. But they managed to rent the trailer next door to us to the biggest crackers on planet earth. Their car horn literally plays Dixie! They have two pigs and not one, not two, but—count them—FOUR fucking pit bulls! There are ten of them living in the trailer. Even worse, they just parked a fucking travel trailer in the driveway over there and there are two more people living there.

I figure Ryan and Jenny did this to see if I would dare to say anything so that they could tell me I'm a horrible person, so I'm damned if I will say a fucking thing. If their fucking dogs get out and come after me or my goats or dog I will quietly shoot them, dump them in the bottoms, and say nothing to anyone about any of it.

It doesn't help that Liz keeps telling me every time the noisy bastards wake us up or keep us up that she told me we should buy the kids' place. Buy it with what? She is getting ready to retire and we are already barely making our bills.

Still no word on when the EMDR therapy device will get to her office. Apparently it is on backorder again. Just my luck. I can tell from the look on Olivia's face that she isn't looking forward to this session. I don't care. I have no one else to talk to and certainly no one I can just say what I think to.

"Those fucking crackers kept us up till one o'clock in the morning with their fucking country western shit station cranked as loud as it would go as they fought with each other over what I have no fucking idea. At this point I wish Ryan would just go ahead and tell me off already and quit punishing me like this. Hell, I have worked my ass off to make my place beautiful, and now I can't sit in my yard because my whole yard smells like pig shit. That's right. There is nowhere on my entire farm where it doesn't smell like pig shit.

"I was almost there in that really good spot I was in a couple of years ago, but then... Well if I'm honest I lost it and feel worse than ever. I'm fucking tired, tired of everything—all of it."

"What do you mean when you say all of it?"

"I mean all. Tired of going to bed at night and waking up in the morning. Tired of everyone and everything, but mostly I'm tired of the only thing that is guaranteed in life is that if I work hard I will get tired. I'm fucking tired of being tired.

"My son hates me so much he rented his property next to mine to the worst crackers on planet earth. We have a crappy president, Senate and Congress. My career is now officially over. My health sucks. I get through one disaster then the next one hits and it feels personal. Maybe it shouldn't, but it does. It feels like the Universe goes out of its way to crap on me. I know it isn't true, but that's the way it feels—you know, like shit. I feel like shit."

I sigh and even to me it sounds like I'm just done. "Sometimes I'm just so tired of being the whipping boy that I lash out. I need people to admit when they are wrong. They don't and so I will then take that anger and attack them. I do this to my wife all the time. Here's the thing. I have been with her for twenty-six years and known her for thirty. In all that time I can count on the fingers of one hand all the times she has admitted she was wrong about anything. So attacking her because I want her to accept blame for any of our problems? It's a waste of time. All it does is piss her off which ultimately makes me so mad that I wind up showing my whole entire ass, and then I have to apologize to her. The fact that she was wrong in the first place evaporates completely and I'm soaking in a pool of guilt because I overreacted."

"Why do you think you overreact?"

"She snaps at me for everything. I can't remember the last time she was actually nice to me. I'm drowning; I need someone to throw me a line. I feel like she is stepping on my head as hard as she can. I have a perverse need to make people wrong so that I can be right. In fact, I'll just be honest I probably need this more than other people because my go-to is to blame myself for other people's bad behavior. And why is that? Because I was programed that way. My dad never once apologized for beating me or for arranging a marriage for me with a thirty-four-year-old pervert. Certainly Levi never admitted to any wrongdoing ever. I was told by them that everything that ever happened to me was my own fault."

"But you know it wasn't your fault, right?"

"The logical part of my brain does. But if it wasn't my fault, why am I the only one who feels like crap? They are both dead; why can I still hear every crappy thing they ever said to me? If there isn't anything wrong with me, why am I alone being punished for the things they did to me?"

"It wasn't because of what was broken in you. They behaved like that because of the broken parts of them that they never fixed."

"And you know what I believe? My father did feel sorry for the things he did. I believe he was tortured, but Levi... Levi loved nothing better than other people's pain. He delighted in the pain he caused women especially because he so hated his mother. He never felt sorry for any evil he ever did; he felt justified. I need to forgive him, but I can't because I am still soaking in the crap he did to me because the lasting legacy he has left me is that my son detests me.

"Dad wasn't a bad man. He had problems of his own. Ryan isn't a bad man at all. He has made huge mistakes which we all have paid for many times over—none more than him. He does and says the things he does and says to me so that I can carry his pain for him. It's not right, but I get it. But Levi—he just needed a whipping boy and I was a great one because I had already been broken in. Why did he drug me and then he and his friends do whatever they wanted to me? He did it to make me dirty, to make me do something wrong so that he could then do whatever he wanted and treat me however he wanted. He needed to make sure that I believed that I didn't deserve better.

"He did it because he was a wall-eyed, drug-addled mess. It was never about me, yet I carry the scars that he created. Where is the justice in that; where is the balance? Why should I even get up in the morning and try to do anything when nothing I do matters to anyone?"

"Does it matter to you?"

"If I'm honest, no. Nothing I do matters to me anymore."

"Forgiving someone doesn't mean you have to be around them or trust them or love them."

"I know. And he's dead, right? He can't hurt me anymore, except... oh wait a minute! I already told you he has driven a wedge between me and my son and that affects everyone I care about. It keeps me from seeing my grandson as much as I want to, it taints my whole life, and he used his death to make sure I could never be at peace."

"Your son says he needs to talk to you. Maybe it's time you forced that meeting instead of just hedging him and dreading it."

"I was afraid you were going to say that."

Chapter Thirteen

The people who pull themselves out of abuse and neglect and become hugely famous, rich, or just successful, or have kids who grow up and respect them and make them proud, those successes can un-program all the bad feelings you ever had about yourself. They will give you worth and put all the demons of your past to sleep.

Unfortunately, most artists of any kind will never have any of this, which is why they are all so crazy. Pursuing the arts didn't make us crazy; we already were. We needed to get huge so that people would have to love us, respect us. When it works it fixes everything. Problem is it doesn't often work. Those of us who never make it, well it isn't because we don't deserve to. I have worked harder and longer than any person who made the big time as a writer. What I didn't have that they did was just dumb-ass luck and... you can't just buy a big jar of that.

For people like me working without a net, with no education or hope of getting one, the arts is our only chance to dig our way out of the pit. But when we fail— and most of us do—the hole only gets deeper and the dark darker.

This is when you need people in your life who will pull you out of the dark, people who can make you feel worthy and loved completely, cared about.

Good luck finding those. I'm fifty-nine, and since we moved away from my granny when I was four I don't think I have ever felt that... except from Ryan when he was little and Avy now.

I just need to feel like anything I do, anything I have ever done, actually matters. I just want my son to love and respect me in a way he hasn't since his shit father first started to manipulate him into believing that all wrong things were done by and are because of me. I needed Ryan to respect me enough to listen to me so that I might have stopped him from making all the stupid mistakes I made and twelve I never even thought of.

I'm not going to set the world on fire; I get that. But would it kill the Universe to throw me a bone, to give me something to hold on to?

Just give up?

I'm afraid to really even try to understand what that means. If I give up doesn't that make everyone who hated on me right? Doesn't that prove that I am actually worthless? Do I not have to keep pushing to try to do something that will make even one person think, "Thank God she was born or XY or Z never would have happened and we'd all be worse off." Will someone please tell me what the hell I can do so that I could actually make enough money—not just to pay my bills but also someone else's—to help my family, maybe send someone to college—maybe my grandson. What if I could make just enough money to put a good roof on my house? That would be nice. What if I could fit my roof with solar panels and at least then my electrical needs wouldn't be part of the problem?

Is that what I have to give up on? You know, every fucking thing?

Perhaps it's as simple as giving up on the idea that I can do anything that matters, that I have some kind of purpose. I don't have to do anything at all, do I?

You can't help other people out of the ghetto of life if you never got out of it yourself. Some people do and they go on to do great things. Many won't even try to get out; they are happy to stay where they are where no one expects anything of them. They are happy to live off others. But many, many people will do everything in their power. They will have great talents and a lot to give to the world. They are hard workers; they never give up, and yet they also never get out of the ghetto. Their voices will never be heard. They will never be able to do any of the great things they want to. They will never get to put solar panels on their roofs, and a lot of them—like me—will have tarps for a roof and just be glad that it isn't raining in the living room... you know... today.

That's right. In a bad wind storm last week a piece of tin the renters had thrown between the big trailer and their travel trailer—so that they could walk between the two houses in the rain—blew off and slammed into our roof putting a head-sized hole in it. I threw a tarp on it, but my legs are way sketchy still and I have no idea when I will be able to actually fix it because honestly because of the angle my feet were on the roof it was all I could do to tack the tarp down.

Maybe the Universe has a reason for keeping me low, for making sure I don't rise above my station, making me the person at the end of the street with the tarp for a roof.

Our lovely new neighbors laughed when they came to get their tin and said, "Damned wind, am I right?" Then they walked that tin right back over to the trailers and put it right back where they had it. Then I was thinking I wouldn't just shoot their dogs and dump them in the woods I might shoot THEM and dump THEM in the woods—and their stinking mother-fucking pigs.

Maybe all I am is an example. I mean, think about it, if all the bright, shiny people who get out of the ghetto come back and inspire people to get out, how much more so the person left behind who makes an oasis in the filth. That rap, sports, movie star... well people may hear their stories and want something better, but while some of them will lift themselves out of the pit of their raising most of them will not. Maybe that's why I'm stuck at the bottom because I can make more out of the nothing I have than most. Maybe other people are inspired by the fact I always do the best I can and make the most of what I have. What if what I do is important, just maybe not to Ryan or to me?

Nope, see that sounds like bullshit to me. It's the kind of thing I tell myself to get through a day, but it never really rings true because there is NEVER any positive feedback. You know when people comment on something I have busted my ass to do? When they don't like it, that's when. Otherwise they say little or nothing. I hate the phrase "That's nice." To me "nice" is something you can get at the hardware store for five bucks. You know, a fifty-pound bag of "nice"—you get it, bring it home, and sling it around your yard and it is magically mowed, all pests die, and a garden grows. "Nice" is something you can just have with a limited amount of work. What I do is not "nice"; it's fucking fantastic because I did it with the crap I dove in the dumpster to get and a bunch of old pallets.

Is it really a problem of my perception; is it that the negative is so loud it drowns out any positive? Or in fact is it just that I hear the negative more loudly?

If nothing I do is important, then what is important? Is it working hard all day and spending all your money on drugs and making everyone in your life feel like crap, ruining not just your life but the lives of everyone around you? Is that important? I let a prescription-drug addict define me. I let people who wanted nothing more than to keep me down, or hurt me in the moment define me till I can't define myself in any but the most negative terms.

My son told me nothing I did was important, and I believed him because that's the same shit his father and my father told me. I believed it because I was never able to pull myself out of the pit and do something that would prove myself worthy not to me but to the world at large. I tried and tried and nothing I ever did was good enough to me because it was never good enough to everyone who told me I was "less than."

My ex got something I always wanted and have never had—the respect my son should have for me and doesn't.

My grandson has changed towards me. The great love he had for me; it isn't there now. My therapist said he has to distance himself from me, that it is how he is dealing with the separation. But now when he could be with me, most of the time he goes to the other grandparents' house, no doubt because they aren't sad. I try not to be sad when I have him, to just enjoy being with him, to be fully present. But it's hard because I feel broken inside. When I have him all I can focus on is when I won't.

Logic can be a bitch. I am completely, debilitatingly broken because of my son's choices. He acts as if I have done something wrong because I have feelings. Therefore the way I feel must be wrong. *I* must be wrong.

God's love comes without caring. God's care has to come from within us. If we don't love ourselves we will never feel the caring love of God, and love without caring will never help us feel better when we are drowning in a sea of our own pain.

I need someone who feels my pain and is willing to put their own desires aside for just a moment to actually help me when I most need it. I need someone who hears my cries for help even when I'm silent, someone who understands me. Without that I don't care what exercise I try or how many times I tell myself "I love me," I will never believe it.

Olivia told me to force a meeting with my son. I wasn't able to do it. I tried. I'd had Avy for a night and day. I was to bring him home by four o'clock Saturday afternoon, and I thought I would just ask my son if he was ready to talk. But when I got there Levi's widow was there visiting. In fact, it turned out I had to have Avy back by four o'clock so he could visit with her. Me, I have to nearly get written permission in triplicate to see the grandson I mostly raised, but this woman who is related to *none* of them, well she gets red-carpet treatment. My son and his wife made it clear they didn't really want me to stay, so I didn't.

I decided Olivia was wrong and I wasn't going to "force" the conversation. Turned out I didn't have to. Two days later my mother called. She needed help; a windstorm had broken a tree in her driveway. So I grabbed my chainsaw and went to cut it out. When I got there my son was there with his tractor. Mother had called him, too. I cut the tree; he hauled it off. Just as we finished... well, that was when he let me have it. That's right; he didn't actually want to talk to me. What he wanted to do was yell at me.

"Mom, I need to get some things off my chest."

When someone says this, what they are really saying is, "Hey I have some things I'm carrying that are making me feel bad, so let me put all of my shit on you so that you can feel bad and I won't have to."

Before he said anything more—and while I was just standing there wondering how to deal with the giant ball of angst that was consuming my entire chest cavity— behind him future me pops up wildly waving my arms around and screaming.

"Give up! Give up! Give up!"

Then the hateful apparition was gone.

But I knew what that meant. This was the moment that I screwed the pooch. I had to tread carefully.

"Your divorce wasn't Dad's fault. It wasn't his fault you were gay. You got a divorce because you were a lesbian."

Nope, that's not why. Not why at all. I would have stayed with him and just been miserable the rest of my life if he hadn't done drugs, flipped out, and almost died in the house on a day I was at work. It was only a miracle that a neighbor instead of our son found him mostly dead. I was tired; sick to death of doing everything, of supporting a drug addict, and didn't want my son to ever be in a position again where he might come home and find his father's bleeding body.

But I said nothing because at least in that moment I knew exactly why my future self was screaming at me. This absolutely wasn't about me. His father had done a horrible thing to him. He spent weeks—knowing he was dying—finishing the task of turning my son against me, and then he shot himself in the head while my son was in the house just to seal the deal. My son needed someone besides himself to blame, and as always I was the go-to whipping boy.

What did I tell him using a secret reserve of calm I didn't know I had? "Your father knew I was queer; that's why my father had him marry me."

He seemed to think on that. You see he knew that was true because his father had told him that a long time ago. It obviously messed with Levi's new story that he told as he was dying—the one that made him look like the one who was abused.

"Well he never abused you."

I said nothing, nothing at all. What could I have said?

"Well he didn't."

"Alright."

"Why does there have to be anything wrong with you? You have PTSD. What the hell from—being a control freak? Why are you such a hypochondriac? He didn't do anything to you!"

"You will believe what you want to believe."

"He never tried to make me hate you."

"Really? Because from the very moment you began to comprehend words he told you in a million different ways that I was stupid and didn't deserve your respect."

Turned out even that was too much for me to say. And so my only son spent an hour and a half telling me every single thing he thought I had ever done wrong to him so that I could apologize yet again. Then he yelled about all the terrible things I did to his poor, poor saintly father who killed himself only so that Ryan could go home to his family.

By the time he had finished his raging fit I felt as beat up and abused as I did when my father beat me; as naked and filthy as when Levi drugged me and then he and his friends used me for party sex.

I swallowed whatever pride I had in reserves and kept my mouth mostly shut until he said, "Why didn't you think I could take care of my own son?"

"Because you were on drugs and at work and your wife was on drugs and flat didn't want to do it."

And then for the first time in years I saw my son. He smiled at me and said, "Well there was that. But why were you always there running around doing things?"

"Because I grew up with a screaming, bi-polar alcoholic. I have spent all my life running around trying to fix things before they break because then maybe everyone would be happy."

"Mom, how would that work?"

"Well... I didn't say it was sane."

He actually started to laugh, and then I did, too I shrugged.

"Look, I'm not going to defend myself. There are two sides to every story. You will decide what is true, what isn't, and what you decide won't match either my version or your father's. I am broken. I know that I do the best I can. Sometimes it is good enough; most of the time the world lets me know it isn't, but then like a fucking weeble I pop back up again. It is never and was never my intention to hurt you in any way, shape, or form."

He hugged me I hugged him. We talked about stupid shit and had a few laughs, and then I went home and fell to the very bottom of the pit and stayed there.

"But didn't you talk it out?" Olivia asked.

"Did you not hear the story I just told you? He told me what a horrid piece of shit I was for an hour and a half. I apologized for being a horrid piece of shit, and now I can't stop looping. I haven't really slept; I feel like crap. Every noise makes me jump. I'm worse than ever, but he's talking to me again and seems to be happy with me. You know, because I let him verbally beat the dog shit out of me. I'm tired of doing the right thing and having it work out for everyone but me."

"The machine is here. Now all we are waiting on is my credentials."

Yes, I still wasn't getting the therapy she said I needed yet.

People who aren't broken never understand what's wrong with someone who is. See, what they don't realize is that at least one person, at least once in their life, told them they were good and worthy, capable and loveable. That person didn't just say these things they showed them with their actions. People who come from families where they are given a sense of worth just for being, just for showing up, they will never understand why you can't just love yourself out of your funk. Why you can't just tell yourself how wonderful you are and go on as if nothing has happened. They don't understand why you can't un-break your own heart. They might have some compassion for your pain, but they will never understand it.

To come from a family where I wasn't valued, where when I was still a kid I was put into a marriage where I was treated as sub-human, and then for the icing on the cake to have an addicted child. Where was my happy, carefree time? I never had one.

Absolutely the worst thing alcoholics—addicts of all kinds—do to the people that love them is that they turn us into codependents. Codependency is a state of being in which we are constantly reacting to the negative stimuli they bring into our life, and you know what? THEY blame us; they think we are making their lives hard. We are trying to keep them from making huge holes in their lives—or worse yet killing themselves and neglecting and abusing their entire family—and they brand us the bad guy. "I wouldn't be a junkie, alcoholic, have a house filled with crap, or weigh six-hundred pounds (whatever their go-to lie of the moment to protect whatever their addiction is) if you didn't ruin my life." It's your fault; you didn't buy them a pony; you failed them; you wouldn't stop meddling.

If I change my perspective just a bit I can see that my son doesn't think I'm worthless, he thinks I'm a pain in the ass. Why am I a pain in the ass? Because he was an addict and addicts always, always, always blame the people they have made codependent. I'm a pain in his ass because I'm codependent, but I'm codependent because he made me that way... Well, him and his father and my father.

Addicts always blame the people they have forced to clean up their messes. They abuse you because you are there. You try to help them; they accuse you of meddling. You try to fix them because you can't fix your life until you fix theirs; you can't fix theirs. They tell you that you are ruining their life as they are actually ruining their own lives and yours, too.

They say don't blame the addict, blame the disease, but then society and the addict... they want to blame the codependents. It's our fault; we should love more and care less. You know... be like God.

There are many definitions for codependency; I like mine. Codependency—the state an addict forces his loved ones into when they have to deal with the fallout caused by the addict's bad choices.

The fallout from dealing with an addict can last years after an addict gets clean. So far I have yet to shake what living with Dad or Levi did to me, and I don't know how long I am going to have to deal with the fallout from Ryan and his wife's addictions. Keeping Avy involved, safe, and happy... running around trying to do anything at all that might make Ryan happy. I'm running on empty. I dropped everything else in my life and now that they have moved and taken Avy, what's left? My marriage took a back seat, my half-assed career, this farm, everything and now... Well nothing is as important to me as Avy and taking care of him, but I don't have that job anymore.

Jenny and Ryan might keep him away to be hateful, but that isn't why they moved. They moved to try to start over and have a better life. I appreciate that but hate what it has done to my life.

You can't concentrate on what you want or need when you are keeping the addict from drowning in their own vomit or tearing your house apart with a sledge hammer. You can't relax when they are constantly pulling you into their drama. And you can never really relax because they could always start using again.

The worst thing an addict does to you is turn you into a fucking codependent, and good luck not becoming codependent when the addict is your child or a parent. From the moment Ryan was born it was my duty—mine because the sainted father was always too fucking self-centered, lazy, and stoned to do anything at all—to take care of him. I loved him with every fiber of my being; that doesn't change because they are in a drug-induced rage screaming hateful things at you and threatening to beat you to a pulp because "You think you're such a bad ass, but you're not a bad ass, and if you don't leave me alone—you know to keep slinging his head into the wall of his garage—I'm going to kick your ass."

Ahh! Memories!

Remember in *As Good As It Gets* when Jack Nicholson says, *You aren't so pissed off because you had such bad childhoods. You're pissed off because other people had it so good. They have memories of picnics by the lake with noodle salad. Yes, good times and noodle salad. Just nobody in this car.* It's not an exact quote nor does it pretend to be, but if you saw the movie, you remember what I'm talking about.

And it's absolutely true. That IS what pisses me off. When you are a codependent person, you don't have happy memories of picnics at the park with noodle salad. You have the night your dad threw the telephone through the living room window, or the morning he busted the kitchen sink with a bar stool. You remember every horrid word he ever said and every beating you ever got, and all of the good stuff gets buried in a sea of his rage. You have shadows of a moment that swims in your brain and you kick yourself for being so stupid as to trust anyone at all, and you wonder how complicit you were in your own rape because you were drugged out of your gourd and your memories are vague. I have memories of going to rehab, and many trips to the hospital, and my son screaming that he hates me.

Those are the lovely memories that addicts give their codependents. I love my son and grandson in a way I have never loved anyone or anything else. So when Ryan did things that could kill him or that might put Avy at risk, my son's—"Stay out of our lives; it doesn't affect you!"—just isn't true at all.

The only way your ungrateful, hate-filled, drug-addled child will ever understand how you feel or what they put you through is if they have a child who is an addict. But you sure as hell don't want addiction for your grandchildren, so the chances are your addicted child will never admit to—much less understand—the gaping hole they alone put in your life.

His addiction was not my fault. I hate drugs. I have ever since the lovely father-creature bullied me into smoking pot laced with God alone knows what then he and his friends took turns on me like I was a carnival ride. If Ryan wants to blame someone for his addiction, he should blame his father. Of course now the bastard went and killed himself "so Ryan could go home," so he can't be blamed or held accountable for anything—ever.

I know Ryan's addiction was not all my fault even if he doesn't. The hateful way he has treated me because of his addiction... I don't blame his addiction; I blame him. No matter what the shrink in his rehab said, he chose to do drugs and therefore the things that he did because he was doing them? Well those are also his fault. Not mine—his.

Ryan is clean now. I once hoped there would be a point in time where he would realize that he owed me at least as big an apology as the one he gave the guy at work who he screamed at one day. Instead he hammers on me for an hour and a half just to make himself feel better.

The self-help books say I don't need the apology of the person who abused me to stop blaming myself. I guess I am defective beyond repair because I actually do need it. I won't get it, but I need it. At least once in my life I need someone who used and abused me to say out loud and to me, "I'm sorry I hurt you. I was wrong."

Just once!

Of course the lovely super-rich spiritual gurus will be quick to tell you it isn't my soul or spirit that needs that apology; it's my ego. You know that bruised, battered, shriveled thing that lives in my hind brain.

Addicts ruin your life whether they want to or not. It isn't their intention, but they do NOT care. Even when they are well they will still not care because it was after all your choice to derail your life to try—and that's the big thing it's just trying not doing—to save theirs. Your life becomes the collateral damage of their disease.

At the end of the day I have to find myself worthy of respect if I am going to keep people from disrespecting me. As long as I don't love or care about myself I'm going to allow other people into my life who treat me like crap.

I know better. It's the doing I'm having trouble with.

I'm not crap. I am actually a pretty amazing person. God alone knows what I might have been able to accomplish if I hadn't been raised by a bipolar alcoholic father, married off at sixteen to a thirty-four-year-old pervert, or wound up with a son who was an addict for twelve years. Considering that I never got the real help I needed to accomplish any of the things I wanted to, and that I have worked every crap job you can imagine and never made decent money even once, I've done pretty well for myself. You know I've always paid my bills, and I've never killed anyone.

It's easy to accomplish great things when you had a good start in life, parents who loved you enough to make you feel special, better yet got you a good education or helped you go into business. Folks who gave you a leg up on life, who helped you be the best person you could be. Without that you can accomplish great things if someone other than family sees your worth and rushes to lift you up. Hard work and perseverance will only ever take you so far without someone to help you, and even then without a big dose of double-strength luck, you might end up like me. Add dealing with an adult child with addiction and there goes the rest of your life.

There was never a time in my life when I didn't have to deal with difficult people and their problems. There was never a time when I could just focus on what I really wanted or needed because I was always responsible for other people, for taking care of what they wanted or needed. Everything I ever wanted for myself was always seen as either useless or selfish by the people who should have—but never did—support me, and now what? What do I do now?

Teach people not to make my mistakes. Maybe that's how I could make a living—giving talks on how not to end up like me.

"Don't get married. Don't have kids. Be super selfish. Always put yourself and your wants first. Do you have talent? Well guess what? No one cares about your talent, and chasing a career in the arts is most likely going to send you into therapy where of course they won't be able to treat you because they aren't certified yet and then they don't have the machine and then they don't have their paperwork. Instead sit on your ass all day watching sappy-assed Hallmark movies. In short, don't be like me."

I admit it. When I had both my legs broken and my whole world was falling apart I did only those chores I could hobble around and do and then... I spent all the rest of my time sitting on my ass watching nothing but fucking Hallmark Christmas movies. I know that's shocking. I mean after all I'm a dyke and a Jew. It doesn't seem like something I would do. But here's the thing: you don't have to worry that it's going to have an unhappy ending. Most of the men are written so effeminately that they might as well be dykes. You can silence it through the freaking Christian music. There aren't going to be thousands of explosions and a lot of angst. For someone with PTSD they are damn-near perfect. I couldn't do my go-to when the world is imploding around me—which is to work myself into a coma—because hello both my legs were broken. Watching those movies kept me from thinking about everything that was wrong. So, thank you Hallmark channel.

By the way, has anyone told Hallmark that there is a war on Christmas? I'm thinking not because they have at least two channels showing nothing but Christmas movies from sometime before Halloween till mid-January—and the entire month of July.

It was in fact July, and Hallmark was still showing Christmas movies. I was sitting on my ass watching one when future me placed her happy ass between me and the TV. I actually moved my head to look around me; that's how much I didn't care what I had to say to me.

"Hey, ass hat, aren't your legs healed now? Even your ankle is healed again, but your roof still has a tarp on it."

"My legs—especially my ankle—hurt too much to climb around on the fucking roof. Besides, nothing I do matters. I'm just going to go through the motions, do just what I have to do, and run out the clock."

"You're going to die."

"Sooner than later I hope."

"Why can't you just give up?"

"I have; this is me giving up."

"You know this is not what I mean."

"Well then tell me what you *do* mean and get the hell out of my way. You are going to make me miss the obligatory Christmas tree lighting—you know that kid is going to be the only kid in town and he will be called to push the button that lights the tree."

"Just give up!" she yelled in frustration, and then she was gone.

"Damn! I missed it," I said out loud, and then I picked up the remote and went back so I could watch it. At that point Liz walked into the room and lost her mind.

"What the hell, Brenda! You have seen that same movie at least six times, and there is a fucking tree lighting in every single one of these movies. Are you ever going to do anything but sit on your ass and watch sappy movies!?"

"You're one to talk." I don't even turn around to face her. "When is the last time you looked up from that stupid candy crushing game in six months? Why is my doing nothing worse than you doing nothing?"

She had retired now. It really hadn't set in yet because of course she was always off for the summer months.

"You have got to stop sleeping, eating, and living your depression. Get your head out of your ass and..."

I jumped out of my chair and spun on her—so I guess it's safe to say my legs were healed. "And do what, Liz? What the hell do you want me to do, what?!"

"Go and write something, anything but nothing. We don't go anywhere, we don't do anything."

"All of the sudden you want to go places and do things. For twenty-five years I'm the one who is dragging you around and you never willingly want to do a fucking thing from screw to go to a fucking movie, and now what... all of the sudden I don't feel like doing anything and you're a fucking party doll?"

She actually walked over, put her phone down on the coffee table then swung around quick like which... well it was Liz, so that's like anyone else doing calisthenics. "You know I have to be talked into things. Once I get wherever you want to go I'm fine. It's what we do; it always has been."

"Well guess what, Liz? I'm tired of dragging your ass around. I'm tired of being the one to always start things. I'm tired of working my ass off for things other people take for granted, tired of not having our grandson, I'm tired of sick goats, and the screwed up roof, tired of always being broke, tired of being everyone's punching bag, I'm tired of feeling like shit. I'm just fucking tired."

"Don't you think I miss Avy, too?"

There are tears in Liz's eyes, and immediately I start to feel bad that I have upset her till I remember that she started this whole thing in the first place. After all I had just been sitting in front of the TV, vegging out, watching crap. Also like I said she had been snapping at me about everything for months, and frankly I was tired of all her shit, too.

"You know what? Until a couple months ago you were at work five days a week. You didn't put him on and take him off the bus. When he was little you weren't with him nearly all day every day and I was. There is a gaping hole in my life, and I feel like I'm dying."

Which was the wrong thing to say, and after we yelled at each other for another thirty minutes she made me an appointment with the doctor. That's right; she decided I was being difficult to live with because I must have a medical problem.

I had started going back to temple, but wasn't going as often. To tell the truth I had tried to go to the *Torah* study group. It is being run by a convert which—that's alright a lot of them know a hell of a lot more than people who were born Jews—but this guy, a nice enough fellow but while he thinks he is fully Jewish he still carries all the baggage from a long life as a fundamentalist Christian. He has encouraged a large number of Christians who want to study to join the group. They are not seekers, they are not attached to Jews, they are Christians who have no desire at all to convert but who want to study with him. I know what Christians believe. If I wanted to be Christian I would be. To me—in the wake of all these shootings—it is like letting the fox into the henhouse. It adds a level of danger we wouldn't otherwise be in, but I am after all super paranoid. Mostly the "leader" wants to keep talking about the end days and how we are in them and... that is super Christian and has no place in a reform shul... and why is he encouraging all these Christians to study with us? Because he thinks they are Jewish souls coming back to the fold.

He lets the Christians tell us what they think during study. I don't care what they think; I'm there to study *Torah* with other Jews. I'm a reform Jew. I don't really believe in the whole "end of days" thing much less that we are in the end times now. I went a couple of times and quit because the "leader" made it obvious that if I couldn't be more understanding of our non-Jewish friends that I needed to keep my female-shouldn't-be-studying-*Torah*-anyway opinions to myself.

I still go some Friday nights though most of the time when I do Liz doesn't go with me, and I never take Avy with me anymore because I don't think it's safe. The congregants say they want me to come more and lead services again, but I'm feeling less and less like I belong there. Less and less like what most of them believe is even close to what I do.

Every day I feel less and less like I belong anywhere at all. I'm thinking about cave living.

While Ryan is at work his lovely renters call. There is a broken pipe. I try to reach Ryan and finally do. He can't leave work; they are in the middle of a crisis; could I please see what I can do—at least shut off the water.

I shut the water off, then I call the crackers and tell them to lock up their dogs and I will see what I can do.

When I get there it is obvious what has happened. One of them pulled a panel out from under the trailer so the dogs would have some place to sleep. The dogs then proceeded to tear up the plumbing. I have to go to the hardware store for parts. It takes me half the day to fix the pipes. As I am screwing the skirting back on the trailer and telling the crackers not to open it again, their fucking drunk brother-in-law opens the door to the trailer. All the dogs run out of the trailer and right over to attack me. The assholes are all trying—without success—to call their pack of attack dogs off of me. I hit one right between the eyes with a pipe wrench and it falls to its knees, but I can't fight off four pit bulls, and I figure I'm dead.

Then I hear a series of gun shots and the dogs all run away. Then I hear Ryan.

"Are you fucking kidding me! My mother comes to fix the plumbing and you let your fucking dogs attack her? I thought I told you to get rid of those fucking dogs!"

The drunk brother in law comes over and decides to yell at Ryan. Ryan is a big guy who works in a saw mill; he's strong as an ox. Don't know if I told you that.

"Who the fuck are you?"

He holsters his gun then palms the guy in the forehead and the guy falls beside the pit bull I hit and is still stunned and whimpering. Ryan looks at the guy he rented the place to.

"There is supposed to be you and your wife here, and what the fuck is that?" he asks, looking at the travel trailer.

"I'm sorry. The dogs wouldn't have hurt her."

"You let your dogs attack my fucking mother. You're trashing out my property. Get your shit and get out."

Then Ryan looked at me. "Are you alright, Mom?"

I was shaking like a dog shitting peach seeds. I looked at my hands. There was a small cut on my finger, but I think that happened when I hit the dog with the pipe wrench.

"Yeah, I think so."

"You can't just evict us," the guys says.

"I can and I will. My mother has PTSD. What the fuck is wrong with you people!?" He got on the phone. "I'm reporting you and your fucking dogs."

"Don't do that, man! We'll move out."

"Oh, you're moving out. I'm still calling he cops."

Ryan put his arm around my shoulders. "Come on, Mom."

He talked to the cops as he walked me back to my house. He was still talking to them as I sat on the porch and when he came back a few minutes later with a bottle of water.

"I'll be next door at my mother's house." He hung up. "I'm so sorry mom," he said.

You know what? I just attached that "I'm sorry" to everything I ever wanted him to apologize for.

"It's all right, Ryan. It wasn't your fault."

He laughed. "You're right; it's fucking Jenny's. She's the one who rented to those assholes. I wanted to rent to my friend Brian, but he was dragging his feet, so… well you know Jenny. I think I'm just going to sell it."

The cops got there and guess what? Three of those fuckers were wanted by the police for various and sundry charges. It did my old, feeble heart good to see them carted out of there in handcuffs and those killer dogs hauled off to the pound.

No, I don't feel sorry for the dogs. They tried to eat my face.

So the cracker neighbors were gone, and my son did actually love me, so things were looking up.

Liz insists on going with me to my doctor's appointment because she is that "worried." In truth I think she went because she figured I wouldn't actually go and then would just lie about it—which if I'm honest is probably exactly what I would have done.

They do a bunch of blood work and in short give me the physical my wife has told me I needed to have since before Avy was born.

The doctor looks from me to my wife. "There is no easy way to say this. Brenda, you are a heart attack or a stroke looking for a place to happen."

"What?" Liz says in a voice that tells me that she really hoping there was actually nothing at all wrong with me.

"Your fasting blood sugar is 306, your A1C is 10 points…"

It was all bad. I was at least sixty-five pounds over-weight, my cholesterol and my triglycerides were super high—no I don't remember the numbers and if you do you should probably get a friggin' life—my blood pressure wasn't bad but not good. In fact, they seemed pretty disappointed my blood pressure wasn't much worse all other things considered, and they just kept taking it until I yelled that it was going to go up for sure if they didn't quit because I was getting seriously pissed off. Nurses always act like taking your blood pressure doesn't hurt, but we all know it actually does and they sure as hell don't need to take it five times in a row.

"You have type two diabetes," the doctor said. He might as well have told me I had leprosy because I could almost see my legs rotting and falling off.

If he had told me I was going to die, well honestly that wouldn't have bothered me at all. Right then I was way ready. You know what I don't want? I don't want to have a stroke and be disabled, to lose a leg, or worse yet—go blind.

He gave me a diet plan and a book to tell me what to eat, how to eat it, and when.

When we got in the car to drive home I turned looked and Liz and screamed what is to me the ultimate conclusion to the hell I have just been handed in color coated spender for my easy understanding.

"This is all your fault!"

"What? How?" Bitch has lived with me for twenty-five years, and it's like she doesn't know me at all.

"You made me go to the doctor. If I didn't go to the doctor; I wouldn't be sick."

"Really, Brenda? That's as stupid as saying if you didn't go to the doctor your legs wouldn't have been broken."

"Maybe they wouldn't have been and that was your fault, too. My life is over! I had nothing, nothing, and now I have to watch every fucking thing I eat! Really, God? As if not eating gluten wasn't bad enough, now I can eat nothing. Fucking crappy shit. And I won't just die. No, if I don't do what they say I'll be a fucking, slobbering, blind-assed cripple."

She was quiet then, like maybe she has finally learned not to try to talk to someone who is losing their ever-fucking mind.

"It's a death sentence; that's what it is—a death sentence. But not an electrocution, not a quick death sentence, no it's a slow, ice pick in the belly wound oozing puss death sentence. That you love!"

"What the hell are you talking about now? I'm not happy you're sick. I'm scared to death, you fucking pain in the ass. Can you just stop being crazy for a minute? This isn't a death sentence; it's a treatable disease that millions of people have and regulate."

"By living a life worse than death!"

"I asked you to stop being crazy."

"That's a lot to ask, Liz. I couldn't take one more thing, not one more thing, and this... this is too much. It's just too much."

"No, this is easy because this is the one crappy thing that has happened in this whole crapfest year that you can actually *do* something about."

"But it's one more thing that sucks, Liz, and I didn't need one more thing that sucks. I just don't need it. I'm not sure I can take it."

She reached over and put her hand on my knee, and I started to calm down.

"You are the strongest person I know. You can do this because you made it through all that other horrid shit, and this... this is just a diet, not the end of the world. And I will do it with you. I need to lose weight anyway."

And just like that Liz was no longer the enemy.

Later that night as I sat vegging out, watching some other saccharin-type movie on the TV, I turned suddenly looked at Liz and said, "Let's buy the kids' old place."

"Okay."

She didn't even hesitate. See, that's what she had wanted to do ever since the kids moved. Then when they rented it to the crackers she really wanted it.

"We can't really afford it."

"We actually can, and I'd rather be broke all the time as have people like that last bunch living next door."

So we bought it and I started working on it, really having no idea what we're going to do with it other than having more pasture and maybe making a bigger garden space and... Well just working on it; having something to do even if I wasn't sure why I was doing it. It was helping me and why... because I knew if I didn't do something my life was going to become all about everything that was wrong with me. Before I would start work for the day Liz and I would sit in the mornings, have coffee, and talk about what I was going to work on for the day. We'd run through different ideas for what to do with the place which had ranged from just fixing it up and renting it to someone of our own choosing to a B&B to a café. We had lots of different ideas, and just having a project we could focus on... well it was helping us both get over our suddenly once again empty nest and bringing us back together.

But I was still struggling when Olivia finally had the green light to start the EMDR treatments. Eye Movement Desensitization and Reprocessing tricks the brain into a kind of REM sleep. In REM sleep the brain processes things and lets them go. In theory it would help me process my trauma and then finally let it go. I would stop looping. I was hopeful, which shocked me because I hadn't had any hope for so long. I think the truth was that I was ready to be healed. I knew it wouldn't fix everything, but I'd worked through the shit once before and got to a good place on my own, and now I was starting to get glimpses of something I knew and lost before.

I had lots to do and my go-to has always been to work harder to keep me from thinking things I didn't want to think. I'm not good at meditation. I do this thing where the moment my mind is even approaching stillness I think, "Wow! I finally did it! That wasn't so hard... Oh wait! Damn, now my mind isn't quiet." Work—especially building things—is the closest I ever get to a real meditative practice.

I wasn't writing but I was building things, fixing things, taking what was broken and making it beautiful again. I was taking the mess my son had made and building something completely different on the bones of it. As I did so it was healing the wound in my relationship with him. We were talking more and more, and he would sometimes come by the house on his way home from work just to say hello and see what I was doing. Not going to lie; I still couldn't let my guard down, but I was starting to feel like we were in a pretty good place.

Chapter Fourteen

For most patients having EMDR therapy, the facilitator has the patient focus on a light bar that lights all the way across and then back and forth to get the eyes to dart back and forth like they do in REM sleep.

"...but you are going to hold a paddle between your thumb and forefinger in each hand," Olivia explained.

"Why?"

"Because you are way too analytical, so I want you to hold the paddles, close your eyes and focus on the traumas of your childhood. Things will come up. Some things you have maybe forgotten, but let them come up and then let them go past. Don't focus on anything. After a few minutes I will stop it and ask you questions about your experience."

I closed my eyes. Shortly first the paddle in one hand would vibrate and then the other and I thought, *What the hell is this going to do?* I started to just focus on the movement of the vibration and pretty soon I realized my eyes were moving with the vibration and I thought, *Cool, I wonder if I can stop it. I just did. NO! She's right; you are too analytical. This is your last chance; let it happen.* So I did what I was supposed to do. I thought about how I felt when I was a kid, and I saw things I had forgotten. The feelings came up, and then they went away. When she stopped me to ask me questions I found there was a moment when I felt like I had to wake myself up to answer her.

It was amazing. After the first treatment—which was four cycles and lasted about forty-five minutes—I felt calm, at peace. I began to find the "normal" I had been chasing my whole life. It felt like a miracle.

It didn't last long. She told me not to annualize it, but of course I did. We are just so incredibly tied to the dreams we made for our life that we can't help but loathe the life we wind up with. I felt better for a minute, but then just had to think about everything that child wanted that they never got.

My life isn't that bad, especially when I look at it in the light of the cluster fuck that it has been. With all that I have gone through and all that I worked so hard at that failed so abysmally, it's amazing I'm not in hock up to my ass, dead, an addict myself, or living in a padded cell somewhere.

But it isn't what I wanted. I just keep settling. I didn't know what I was going to do with the kids' place and... I still didn't have a decent roof on my house and what the hell was I thinking going back into debt when I didn't have a roof on my house?

A roof's expensive, and I'm working with bubble gum and spit to fix the place next door up, but just the payments are going to eat all our extra money. Here's what I know: you never actually have "extra" money. You have money you don't need till something breaks. Then there were the added utility bills which we hadn't even considered when we bought the house. I needed to find a way to make money with the damn place or how could we ever afford it? Wasn't it stupid to think that vibrating paddles could solve my problems when my problems were so big?

I've always just flown by the seat of my pants, going from one disaster to the other, teaching myself as I went along.

But when I could push all those thoughts out of my brain for a minute... after that first treatment I felt better. And I was scheduled for four more. Some people with PTSD only need one treatment. I had a feeling I was going to need all five they had scheduled me for.

I didn't vote for Trump. The things he is doing are NOT my fault, and I guess I really shouldn't blame Jesus either.

I've never been an addict or an alcoholic, and it's not my fault that the people in my life were.

We live in a fucked-up world where we near worship people who steal, go to jail, do drugs or alcohol, and then turn their lives around and become model citizens. We give them scholarships and support and pat them on the back and applaud how well they are doing.

What about all the people who didn't do any of that crap? Where are our book deals? Where are our scholarships? There are a whole lot of people like me who have busted their asses, never done anything actually wrong, and what did we get... a big bucket of slugs, that's what. The ex-addict, -alcoholic, -con gets a ticker-tape parade, but the people who were destroyed by their crappy-assed life decisions, what do we get?

Nightmares, day mares and EMDR therapy for our PTSD. Yay!

Everyone just loves Ryan and are oh so proud of him for turning his life around. I am, too, but... He didn't turn his life around on their heads as he spun them into the ground. Ryan's sobriety has only started to trickle down to me.

Trump's huge tax cut for the rich will never get all the way down here where I am.

The higher power I am supposed to turn my problems over to... I just can't buy it anymore. I am doing better, but my bitterness seems to have taken up residence in my soul. I am resigned to things not really getting better, to just making the best from bad things. I'm not sure that is actually a good thing. I'm staying on my diet and losing the weight. My building projects are helping me cope with my stress and get in better shape.

I need to let go of my bitterness, but how am I supposed to release my bitterness when the Universe—

that wonderful higher power everyone wants to cling to—seems to tell me daily that nothing I do matters? Why can't what I do have merit and worth? I'm scared shitless that my latest project will also fail. I have three months before it has to start making money or we won't have enough to live on. It doesn't have to make a lot, but it has to make something. Since everything I have ever done has failed, why on earth did I think I could do this?

Why do people who do something horrible "fix themselves" and then they are celebrated, but I can't even make enough money to pay my bills? I'm spending money we really don't have to fix up my son's old place, and we still don't have a decent roof on ours and no money to get it and now... I have just made it that much harder for us to get the money to fix our roof right. I wound up putting another tarp on it.

Is my son right? Is nothing I do important? Does he still feel that way or did he feel that way in the moment and won't apologize for what he said—not because he believes what he said was true but because then he feels like I will do to him what he does to me. You know, bring up things he apologizes for because then I will know he feels bad about it.

I am ready to have my next treatment, but it is two weeks away.

My friend Walter called. He and his crew just stripped the steel roof off a shed. "Insurance is paying for all new steel, but Brenda this stuff is like new. If you can come and pick it up, you can have it."

"I'm on my way."

It's a huge pile, so big I have to make two trips, and it is good stuff. As I am loading the last of it on my truck Walter walks over and throws a huge box in the front of my truck.

I give him an odd look and he smiles and says, "Fasteners. They are mixed from different jobs, but..."

"No, that's great! Thank you, Walter! Thank you so much."

"No, thank you. If I get out of here today I get a bonus, and if I had to haul all that shit off I never would have made it."

I stop working on my projects next door and start working on our roof. It's a lot of ladder work and a lot of work period, but get this—Liz puts down her phone and comes outside to hand me pieces of tin. Towards evening on the third day when my butt is about to drag my tracks out, my son comes just to visit. Without being asked he climbs right up on the roof and starts helping me. Just as it was getting dark we are getting down from our new roof. The whole time we are working we are talking and laughing, and it feels like we have turned a huge corner.

He is getting ready to go home and I am thanking him and he says, "You know what, Mom? Thank you. That place looks great. Before you started fixing it up I thought about all the work I did on it and all the work you did and during my addiction it turned into a pit and now—it looks great again. I actually came by to ask you if you could help me fix my deck. See they just painted it before they sold the place and it turns out the whole deck is just a rotten mess. I can't do it myself, so now that I helped you..."

He smiles his most brilliant smile, and I feel reborn.

So I had a new roof, and my son needed me, and my next EMDR treatment made me feel even better.

I helped my son build a new deck on his house. The whole time Avy helped us, and it was a great feeling to have three generations building something together. While we were working on it my daughter-in-law was super helpful, sweet and kind, until I wondered what the EMDR treatment was really doing to my brain—or if she had been abducted by pod people—but either way I was alright with it. When we finished the project we were all sitting on it, talking. My dad had always called what we were doing an "appreciation break." You worked hard on a project then you just sat back, looked at it, and enjoyed that it was done. Ryan went in the house to get some more ice tea.

"How much weight have you lost?" Jenny asks.

"Sixty-five friggin' pounds," Avy answers for me with a smile.

"You know... I never realized how many times I called you for one kind of help or other until we were living here and you couldn't just walk next door. Thank you for helping Ryan with the deck."

I was shocked silent for a minute. I took a deep breath then said, "You're very welcome."

As I was driving home of course I had to analyze it, and I realized what was happening. As long as I was right next door they didn't appreciate anything I did for them. As long as they were sneaking around doing drugs everything I said or did was me "meddling," and it was easy to blame me because I was always there running around trying to keep things from breaking, so everyone would be happy and not yell.

When they didn't have me to blame and they still had problems, they had to admit that not all their problems were caused by me. When they couldn't just call me when they needed help and have me come over, they started to appreciate what I'd done for them. Mostly the further they got away from their addictions, the more they were growing up and becoming the people the drugs kept them from being. My daughter-in-law could still get on the pope's last nerve, but by God she is trying to be a better person. She's working on fixing herself, on her life, and on being a good mother.

But even when things in my personal life were getting better... well, it's hard to not worry because... You know... Trump.

The people who are his staunchest supporters—he has screwed them over completely, but they're just too fucking stupid to know it. You know except for the super-rich people who voted for him—life is going pretty good for them right now. Corporations were already eating the country, but Trump just tied a big ribbon on America and gave it to them. The idiot welfare people who voted for him... they are getting trounced by the weather just like the rest of us, they are paying higher prices at the stores, they don't have better jobs, they aren't making more money, but they don't blame the fat cats or Trump. After all, they are the job makers.

Who do they blame then? They blame everyone but those who are really making their lives harder, but when we call them idiots we are just as big a bigot as they are. Or so they say.

Let me explain for simple-minded folks why calling someone who is an idiot an idiot isn't the same as bigotry. A bigot hates people—not because of anything they have done, but because of who or what they are. If I say I hate bigots, that doesn't make me a bigot, too. I don't hate them because of what they *are*; I hate them because of what they *do*. I hate that they go into black (or African-American) places of worship and shoot people just because they are the wrong color. I hate that they go to temples and kill Jews and they go to WalMart and kill Mexicans. I hate that they want to take my tax money and build a hateful wall. I hate that they are not only alright with separating children from their parents and putting them in concentration camps, but they think it is a righteous act. I hate that they hate me, alright! I hate them because they have hearts filled with hate. I'm old enough to remember the Civil Rights movement and how they beat and killed people just because they no longer wanted to be treated like dogs.

I was raised to be a bigot. My father was a bigot—a weird one. He thought black people—no one else just black people—were lesser humans. I used the N-word I used the N-word because I wasn't allowed to call blacks anything else. If I did, my dad beat the crap out of me for being a "bleeding-heart liberal."

Early in my twenties I realized that everything he had told me about black people was a lie, and I worked to change both my thinking and the words I used. I didn't choose to live my whole life in ignorance. But because of this I can give you a first-hand account of how a racist is created. Bigots are created from the ground up. From the moment they are born their parents feed them a big dollop of hate along with their breakfast cereal. They tell them that all the problems in the world are created by this or that group of people. We believe it because it's our parents telling us this shit, but like everything else—if you get out in the world—if you don't *choose* to remain ignorant—you learn better.

The only people who have ever ruined the lives of others for their own purposes are the rich. The rich keep people from coming after them by dividing us into groups that then hate each other. The ugliest of all ways of thinking is—and always will be—to blame people based not on what they have done to us or the planet, but because of what they look like, the way they pray, or who they love. The rich need us all at each-other's throats because then... well then we put an orange idiot in the White House who slings through policy that will ultimately make us slaves to the corporations. Meanwhile, all that the people who voted for him care about is that he locks up Mexicans, puts blacks, and women, and gays in their "place," doesn't take any of their gun rights away, saves the unborn babies, and kills the whales.

His inability to accept any blame for anything, the inability to say "I'm wrong" just proves what we already know: Donald Trump has narcissistic personality disorder. You know, like every other really dangerous psychopath, he is willing to do horrific things if it gets him what he wants right now. What does he want? To be a god, to be seen as an infallible god—and his followers see him that way. He is for them the way, and the light because he sees that it is all these "mud people" who are ruining everything, and it is all these "mud people" that must go.

Why does he want a fucking wall? Because he knows no one would ever let him have a pyramid made for him. That wall is a monument for him, and what does history tell us, what do we know about this kind of huge, expensive monument? They are empire and environment killers.

The worst kinds of people still support him. Some dumbass people voted for him and are now sorry they did so, but the people who still think he is a "great president" accept that he is a hater, which means they support the hate, which means they are haters. They need to quit lying to themselves and everyone else and just admit to what they are—white nationalists who think they deserve this country more than everyone else. And you know what? They could have it if there was anywhere else for us to go, but there isn't, so... We need to rise up and take our country back.

No idea how to do that. All I can do is go to the polls and vote for the asshole I think will do the least damage...

That isn't Trump. Never was.

Selina Rosen

Chapter Fifteen

I go through all my EMDR treatments, and I finally start to see what it's like to have a brain that isn't eaten up with PTSD. I was starting to mend my relationships with my son and my wife.

By the way, my wife went to the doctor, too. Turned out she had a severe and very dangerous hormone imbalance. That's right. All the snapping at me she swore she wasn't doing—she was—and there was a medical reason for it.

When she doesn't snarl at me and yell at me all the time, well it's much easier to love her.

Nothing was fantastic but everything was manageable. We had a friend who needed a place to live. He rented the house next door even though I'm still not finished with the renovation. He's alright with me working on it when I have to, and the rent he pays us makes its payment and pays its utilities. So we get to have the land to use, he's not just a good neighbor and tenant, but he likes to come some mornings just hang out, drink coffee and bullshit, so he's just about perfect.

We have worked it out with the kids so that we get Avy every other weekend which is working out pretty good.

I'm still not really writing—and by the way I don't consider this writing.

My health was pretty good. I was still fighting depression and still in therapy which sort of pissed me off because I wanted to be better in all ways.

Olivia is looking at her computer screen as I talk. My guess is she was taking notes, but she might have been like Liz playing a game and pretending to work.

"...the economy is better and anyone who says otherwise... well that is fake news. But who is the economy better for? Not me, not for anyone I know. They tell us that unemployment is at an all-time low, but that's mostly because they cut a bunch of government programs and people had to go to work—which isn't necessarily bad Except wait—everyone's working two or three jobs, but no one has any fucking money. We can't pay our bills, and everything in the store is so expensive we can't really afford it, and the rich got a huge tax break but once again nothing but shit is trickling down.

"But as long as they just keep telling us that the economy is strong and unemployment is down the Trump supporters will keep right on supporting because after all it's the liberal's fault they can't pay their bills."

"Is this really what's bothering you?"

"Well yeah. That and people just keep opening fire on people everywhere and no place is safe anymore..."

"What's really bothering you?"

I sigh. "Why am I not healed? I feel much better, but I'm not healed, and I am so fucking tired of watching everything I eat and every dime I spend and..."

"In the last few months you have said no to several people who asked you to do things you didn't want to do. You have lost all the weight the doctor told you to lose and you have improved your health. You have made huge strides in repairing your personal relationships. Hell, you managed to put a new roof on your house. I think you are healed."

"But I'm not feeling it."

"No one feels good all the time."

"Apparently making America great again means making it a place where the rich white guys have everything and the rest of us work all the time to clean up the mess they made. Where the only jobs we can count on don't pay enough to live on and are all about cleaning up the latest storm from the latest climate change disaster—which is of course not the fault of rich industrialists who are all about raping the earth to line their pockets."

"Again, is this really what you feel you need to talk about?"

I took in a deep breath and let it out.

"This morning I woke with a taste of bitterness in my mouth that went all the way to my soul. Nothing I do matters. Nothing. So what's the fucking point of even getting out of bed? The world and especially the United States has become a cesspool, and my own life... well it's better than it was, but it isn't good, and the shit could hit the fan at any minute.

"I can't afford to do anything I want to do. I can't eat a fucking thing I want to eat. I can't fix any of the things I'd like to fix, and I'm just getting older, sicker, and more tired. What the fuck was the point of my life, of my pain, of anything? How did my misery serve anyone or anything, and why do we even try when someone like Trump is getting every single thing he wants? Why does he get the life of his choosing when it destroys so many people, but I can't have a fucking thing I want even though the things I want wouldn't hurt anyone? When what I want would in fact make other people's lives better? The legacy I'd like to leave is one of people being better off for me having been born, not making my own hole in the ozone, not building a huge wall."

"Can you tell me what happened?"

I sigh. It is going to sound stupid even to me, but I say it. "I took my two young goats to be tested for CAE. The results should come in any time. If they have it then everything I have done with my goats for the last two years has been a waste."

"And if they don't, have it you will still have a herd."

"I need something really good to happen, something seriously good so good I can't talk my way out of it.

Something so good it makes me glad I went through all the hell I went through if it got me that great thing. I'm tired of mediocrity disrupted by horror. I want something actually *good* to happen."

"Lots of good things have happened for you in the past year."

"No, lots of mediocre things have happened. Nothing earth shakingly good has happened."

"And it probably won't; you have to let nice be enough."

"You know what might be NICE? Some fucking sleep."

Usually I come home from therapy feeling better, but not that day. No, I could still near taste the bitterness of my soul; it was that bad.

Liz had gone to play bridge, and the house was empty. I sat down in my chair, leaned back and was almost asleep when the phone rang. It's the vet's office, and I cringe; ready for the worst.

"Hello," I say.

I can hear the all-too-familiar sound of dread in my own voice.

Then the woman says, "Miss Gold, your two does tested negative for CAE."

I am shocked silent, unaccustomed to anything remotely good happening.

"Miss Gold, are you there?"

"Yes, thank you, thank you so much."

When I hang up the phone I start to feel really happy for the first time in years, and then I get scared—petrified actually. Why? Because every time I have allowed myself to be really pumped about anything, no matter how small, something catastrophic happens and immediately my brain starts making pictures of all the evil crap that could happen and how I would have to deal with it.

Then there I am standing in front of me. I hadn't seen me for months, and immediately think my EMDR therapy has stopped working.

"We are just fucking hopeless," I tell me. "God, I am such a fucking dumbass. The therapy worked; we're much better. The problem is all us."

"That's not helpful. That's what everyone has always done to me—blamed me because I'm unhappy."

"Listen and learn, dumbass. You are so terrified of joy that the minute you feel the least bit happy you start to put disclaimers on it. You start immediately to think about what horrible thing the Universe is going to do to you to make you pay for even a moment of joy. Just give up!"

"I still have no idea what the fuck you mean when you say that."

She sighs and shakes her head. "No, I never did. Look at me. Really *look* at me—not past me like you have been doing all this time because you are afraid to look at me too hard. Really *look* at me. What do you see?"

"I lose that last five pounds I want to lose to have wiggle room."

"Yet we die anyway. So look harder."

I did, and then I knew. "I don't live very much longer, do I? You aren't much older than I am."

"And what do you think it is that kills us?"

"I didn't give up?"

"Exactly."

"Yet I still have no idea what that means."

"God, I can't believe I was ever this big a dumbass. Give the fuck up."

"Give up on what?"

She starts pacing back and forth. "We know—right now, in this moment—we know *exactly* what we have to give up on, but we just can't even bring it to the front of our mind."

"Just tell me!"

She stops, turns, and looks down at me and yells back, "Everything! Every fucking thing! Give up on the stupid notion that everything has to make sense. Give up on the idea of having to have balance. When you've had the kind of life that we have had, you can't make balance. People like us rarely get the breaks to "succeed," and we spend our whole life just chasing normal. People with the kind of life history that we have... well you're right it would take something huge to balance out the absolute tragedy of our life, and most people just like us they will never get that huge thing. You're right all most people have is horror occasionally interrupted by mediocre moments of temporary joy. The difference between them and us is that they learn to just give up—not on life or on doing things, but on expecting that anything will come along and define their purpose. That there is any way that they can control other people and stop them from hurting them. They don't worry day in and day out about what horrible thing is going to happen next. They actually enjoy good news like "the goats are going to live" without wondering if the Universe is now going to kill a cherished loved one to continue to punish them.

"Just give up on expecting that the karma train is going to stop at your station and reward you for all the good you have done and erase all the bad that has been done to you. Karma is a bullshit thing just like heaven and hell—a promise that somehow good people will be rewarded for good deeds and bad people will get their comeuppance for all the bad they do. It just doesn't work that way. Hello! Trump is President of the United States. Will he be impeached? I don't know; I seriously doubt it, but no matter what happens, you sitting and worrying about how much worse it can get... that isn't going to fix a God-dammed thing. Your daughter-in-law is trying to be a better person, and she is trying to show you that she does appreciate you. You're right; she could turn back into a flaming evil bitch tomorrow, so don't waste right now worrying about if she is going to make your life a living hell again. Just enjoy that she isn't doing it right now. You and your son seem to have gotten back to a good place, so quit being mad at Levi because he caused all this grief and just accept that you lived long enough to get your son's love back in spite of everything he did. Right now there are no bugs in your house."

Something I said without saying it suddenly hit me. Future me didn't know what happened with the impeachment proceedings.

"That's right, asshole, if you don't give up you are going to live just long enough to lose that last five pounds. I know—believe me I know—how hard it is going to be, but you have got to quit worrying about every fucking thing. Learn to deal with crap when it happens and then let it the fuck go. The EMDR therapy gave you the tools to do that. We deserve to live, we deserve to be able to enjoy moments of happiness even joy. Forget about the past and making things balance. Just live right now in this moment, from moment to moment. You know all this shit; put it into practice. Put down your armload of broken dreams and move forward. Stop worrying about who you're going to be, and just be."

Then I was gone and I knew I wouldn't be back, because now I knew everything I needed to know.

The answer was so simple I had already read it in the *Tao* and—in different ways—in dozens of other spiritual books.

Chop wood, fetch water.

Terrible things happen; we can't fix what can't be fixed. Sit in it. Have a good cry. Allow myself to feel my pain; don't deny it. Then get up and chop wood and fetch water.

I'm super happy that my two little goats don't have CAE and I still have a herd, that my family is getting along well, and that there are no bugs in my house. I'm not going to worry about what horrible thing will happen next; I'm not going to wait for the next shoe to drop. I'm going to enjoy when things aren't a crap fest. Not "if" but "when" something horrible happens, I will deal with it and then let that go, too.

I'm going to trust that I can live through whatever the future has to throw at me because after all look what I have already been through.